WHEN THE TYPHOON BLOWS

OTHER BOOKS BY MRS. LEWIS

YOUNG FU OF THE UPPER YANGTZE (Winner of the Newbery
Medal)

HO-MING, GIRL OF NEW CHINA

CHINA QUEST

PORTRAITS FROM A CHINESE SCROLL

TEST TUBES AND DRAGON SCALES (In collaboration with Dr.
George C. Basil)

WHEN THE *typhoon* BLOWS

by

ELIZABETH FOREMAN LEWIS

Illustrated by Kurt Wiese

THE JOHN C. WINSTON COMPANY
Philadelphia
Toronto

To My Son,
John Fulton Lewis

ACKNOWLEDGMENTS

The author is deeply indebted to Dr. Idabelle Lewis Main, of Shanghai, for carefully reading and checking all details in this book; to Mrs. Ralph Ansel Ward of East China, and Mrs. William McCurdy of Chungking, Free China, for special information on the Chinese scene; to Professor Chao-ming Chen for Chinese terminology; to Dr. George C. Basil for medical data; and to Miss Elizabeth Winchester King for invaluable assistance in the preparation of the manuscript.

CONTENTS

Part I. THE ATTACK

Part II. THE REFUGEES

ix

ILLUSTRATIONS

Part 1. THE ATTACK

CHAPTER I

"The Yangtze Never Flows Backward; No More Can Age Understand Youth"

THREE things there were with which Li San-djiu (Li Thirty-nine) had been familiar since his birth—the sea, a boat, and a fort. These, with his grandfather, Lao To (Old Head), a title of respect accorded years and graying hair, had filled the youth's life, and so far he had felt no other need. Old Head provided family; the sea and boat, a living; and the Fort added interest and recreation.

Born on his father's thirty-ninth birthday, the boy had been named San-djiu-tz in honor of that occasion. Eighteen moons later, the swell from a foreign steamer had capsized the

1

family sampan as his parents and an older brother fished from its decks. When the empty craft washed ashore, Old Head, accepting this triple loss with the resignation common to fishing villagers, had taken upon himself the jealous care of the one remaining child of the Li House.

Their first years alone had been difficult indeed for the grandfather. The housewifely tasks of cooking and seeing to the baby's personal needs had been but a minor part of the old man's duties. From an inconstant sea and the small square of sandy soil beside their hut, a living for the two had to be wrested; and on those leaden days when the surf roared its warning to all trespassers, Lao To, laboring with hoe and fertilizer, coaxed discouraged vegetables to grow and bear.

Whether on land or water, he kept the child beside him. Swaddled in cotton-padded garments and securely noosed by a bamboo-plaited thong to a stout peg on the deck, San-djiu, as he was called for short, soon grew accustomed to the sampan's pitch and toss in the grip of tides. By the time he reached his thirteenth birthday, the boy had become as adept as an adult at casting and hauling nets. Daybreak now saw him off with the fishing fleet, leaving Old Head, except on the finest mornings, to the less exacting demands of life ashore.

Alone, the old man moved leisurely about the mud hut attending to household tasks. Often he paused to sit on a stool before the door and soak sunshine into his bones, which were now paying for the toil and exposure of many years. Increasingly, his thoughts centered on the comings and goings of Thirty-nine. No woman had given a hand to rearing this youth, the grandfather would remind himself with satisfaction, and what house in the village could boast a son as capable? Already the boy's skill compared favorably with that of older fishermen; given another year or two his strength, also, would equal theirs, for the young body, lean though it was, possessed stout muscles. Moreover, a full head and a ready tongue lay under his grandson's black thatch of hair. Consider his popularity at the Fort—a thing their neighbors all envied! "Truly, truly," Lao To told himself frequently with a grin from which the front teeth were missing, "among mothers I am good indeed!"

While Li the Elder sat dreaming at home, San-djiu struggled with the sea for treasure. Before noon, he poled to shore, made fast his sampan, and carried the live and shining spoils in a bucket to the hut. There his grandfather helped him grade the catch—reserving the poorest for their own food supply and placing the choicer ones in two battered Standard Oil tins of water. Then, after stuffing down a bowl of rice topped by green vegetable, the youth swung the tins from a shoulder-pole and set out at a steady pace for the Fort.

As competitors hurried past him in the same direction, Thirty-nine smiled to himself. He had long since taken care of trade problems by an occasional small gift of shellfish or seaweed to the cook who was commissary at the Fort. This thoughtfulness, which cost practically nothing, kept him in good standing where it counted most. In return the cook haggled prices with the rest of the group until the youngest among them had arrived.

Ignorant of these donations, the other fishermen were at a loss to understand this open favoritism. Neither sympathy for an orphan nor for a half-grown boy forced to compete with men would influence the Fort's hard-bargaining commissary. When that worthy, it was commonly rumored, finished shaving down an original price, the one who had made it hardly recognized the ghost that was left. True, the soldiers permitted this young one privileges beyond those of other boys in the community—and perhaps their feeling was shared by the cook as well. But whatever the reason, it mattered little. At best, the garrison paid poorly for supplies, and by the time the cook's customary "squeeze" had been deducted, there was little left. Many villagers considered it more profitable to make the long trip into city markets where prices seemed in fairer proportion to effort involved.

On his part, Thirty-nine felt that the extra time and energy used in such journeys balanced small returns in the trading scales. To no one but himself did he admit that there was still another reason for his keeping in close touch with the Fort. His first entry through that forbidding gateway at nineteen months had been in a basket that balanced the tin of fish on the other end of Grandfather's shoulder-pole. As time passed and he grew old enough to walk at Lao To's side, this daily appearance at the barrack became the high point of his life, and the soldiers in turn began to look on the boy as a means of diversion in an otherwise idle existence. For San-djiu this was no easy position to occupy, but he learned early to endure their curses and blows as the price to be paid for the only recreation in his life.

Repeated conquests of the sea had long since dulled the sharp, attractive edge of danger in that quarter. When, in a life of toil and hardship, moments of leisure came, they were limited chiefly to the unexciting companionship of an old man. Affectionately devoted to his grandfather, Thirty-nine nevertheless found tedious in the extreme these conversations based on aged memories or on the familiar happenings of each day. His mind was hungry for adventure, and having nothing else to feed it, fastened on the Fort. Gradually the barrack with its men and arms dedicated to sinister purposes, became the symbol of all that was strange and different in life.

Sometimes on moonlit summer nights, while his young body ached with fatigue and Lao To's voice urging sleep echoed in his ears, he would step outside the hut for another look toward the stout, gray-stoned building. At hand the village lay as motionless and still as any painting on a scroll, its roofs and road a sheet of white marred only by the tattered, sprawling shadows of drying nets. Thirty-nine's gaze swept past the community as if it did not exist. He was too familiar with the drab poverty of life under each thatched roof to have imagination tricked now by any web of transient beauty. Instead, with his bare feet sinking into the sand, he stared into the distance where the barrack gleamed frostily in a cold, silvery setting of sky and sea.

He was aware that the men within its walls were much less useful citizens than his own hard-working neighbors. Their profession, though, was a part of history's pages, and they talked knowingly of towns and cities that were linked with

all the rich tradition of his land. With such subjects he
had only the most limited acquaintance. He could neither
read nor write, and what he had learned of other places and
times had come to him in garbled snatches from Old Head
and their neighbors. In the soldiers' talk, however, past,
present, and future mysteriously merged into one.

Standing there alone in the white night with the sea advancing hungrily on the shore below, he found himself repeating some of the magic names to which the troops so
commonly referred. Peiping, Nanking, and Soochow; Shanghai, Ningpo, and Canton, the words would shape on his tongue
to remind him that somewhere beyond this village Fortune
lay waiting for the youth who would seek it out. Finally the
realities of life would make him turn again to the mud hut
that was his home and there, shut in with darkness, forget
the future in sleep.

In the harsher brilliance of sunlight, illusions faded, and
the glamour with which he had invested the soldiers at night
changed to bare acceptance. For the most part they were a
lazy, shiftless lot that had drifted into the ranks by devious
ways; and he had serious doubts about their worth if trouble
arose. The two small cannon and the store of light arms in
the Fort commanded more of his respect than did the men.
When, as occasionally happened, the youth was permitted to
handle a rifle, he felt a swift indignation at signs of neglect
in oiling and polishing.

One afternoon Old Head squinted attentively at his grandson and remarked, "Your left cheek is the yellow green of a
typhoon sky."

Thirty-nine nodded. "One of the men struck me because I rubbed rust from his gun. To trust fine weapons to those worthless *mah-pai*-playing (gambling with dominoes) pigs is foolish indeed!"

"Even more foolish is it to meddle in other men's affairs! Moreover, how do you know when a gun is rusty or when it is not?"

"I have watched some of the better men clean theirs until wood and metal shone like silk." He paused as if searching for words to explain his feeling. "Perhaps seeing those lazy fellows careless with weapons more valuable than they are, fires my anger; fishermen learn early to care for their nets."

"The poor man cannot afford anger for a plaything," Old Head reminded, then rising from the table, began to settle things for the night. Later, wrapped in a patched *pu-gai* (a comfort stuffed with cotton wadding), he wondered anxiously about his grandson's future visits to the Fort. It was true that the men were a worthless lot, and some day bad temper added to idleness might lead to worse than mere blows on the cheek. For him to understand the youth's interest in the building was different. He, himself, instinctively wary of anything to do with war-making, had never thought of the barrack, except as a place in which to transact business promptly and leave. But Thirty-nine—*ai-ya*!

Almost as soon as this fear of Lao To's developed, it died. "What happens that you now manage your affairs at the Fort so swiftly?" he asked his grandson one afternoon several weeks later.

San-djiu smiled. "At present no one there has leisure to waste on me. Truly you would never recognize the place. All the old officers are gone, and these new ones from the Central Government at Nanking make the soldiers work as hard as if they were honest men earning a living."

Lao To, tying a knot with his netting-needle, commented dryly, "For soldiers to work is odd indeed, but of what use except in battle?"

"That I asked the cook," Thirty-nine replied. " 'I have no time for questions,' he told me crossly, but when I presented him with several crabs, his tongue loosened a little. 'It is important that all in this place be properly trained; by no other means can we keep the enemy from taking more of our land!' "

" 'What enemy?' I wanted to know."

" 'Who else but the Japanese?' answered the head of the kitchen. 'Have they not already robbed us of Manchuria and the Northern provinces? If we do not stop them now, we shall soon cease to be a nation.' Then he added, 'Though why I should learn a second time to cook is hard to understand. Morning and evening these new officers inspect my kitchen and order me to study the rules in that little book on the shelf. Food bowls are not to be cleaned with a damp rag, I am told; instead, they must be dipped carefully in boiling water. When I ask who is to pay for so much water and the charcoal to heat it, they tell me to put the cost into my accounts. Thus have I done, but when they see the silver spent during this moon, they may not be so hothearted about the matter!' "

Old Head suddenly interrupted his grandson's narrative. "Early I learned to expect some foolishness from every government; these rules, however, are silly beyond belief."

His grandson grinned. "Wait, Old One, until you hear what followed! 'Thirty years,' the cook continued, 'I have prepared food for other men to eat; now, for the first time, I must wash fruit and green vegetables in the red foreign drug (permanganate of potash) that the men may not be sick. As if water and drugs harm disease demons! Moreover, why waste medicine on the vegetables when it is the men who should drink it? One question I would ask the Central Government—am I a doctor or a cook?'"

"Can I trust my own ears?" exclaimed Lao To, then he added thoughtfully, "these ways will pass. In another moon the new officers will be like all before them; rules will be forgotten, and the troop will do as it has always done in the past."

In this instance Experience was a poor prophet. Moons rose and waned, but conditions at the Fort continued to improve. The dominoes, not the books of rules, lay covered with dust, for gambling and brawling had become things of the past. Sharp drilling commands and the clop-clop of feet in formation echoed on the air from dawn to dark. The barrack itself was clean as never before in history, and reflections from polished weapons threw points of light into the darkest corners. For the first time in several generations, soldiers and civilians alike were being roused to national consciousness by the sudden imminence of a danger long since foreseen.

Months became a year, and on the eve of his fifteenth birthday, Thirty-nine informed Lao To with satisfaction, "Today, after selling my fish I stood in the road to watch the men drill. That they are the same fellows I have always known is beyond belief."

Old Head's eyebrows lifted cynically at the last statement. "Whether they seem good or bad is of little importance now; when trouble comes, you and I still must fight for ourselves."

"Naturally! the Generalissimo expects every citizen to do his part. At present our people are uniting, for the country needs all of us."

"The Generalissimo! The country!" mocked Lao To. "*Tao-tih* (down to the ground) Government expects peaceful men to help! That is always the way, as any babe knows. If the 'black dwarfs' or some other rule in this land, it matters not; taxes will be the same for fishermen and farmers."

"The Japanese shall never have this land!" San-djiu began hotly, then said no more. Even a year ago, he admitted silently, I myself cared little about what happened to the nation. Old Head and his contemporaries, having lived under a succession of greedy and indifferent governments, could not possibly understand officials and ordinary citizens working together for the common good. In this new and broader plan even the humblest man was important to the country's welfare, and the youth had no doubt that when the expected trouble came, he himself would be equal to the moment's demands.

Even word of actual attack left Grandfather undisturbed. "The enemy has seized Marco Polo Bridge," Thirty-nine announced excitedly one day on return from the Fort, "and yesterday fighting began at Shanghai."

"Well, what is a bridge or even Shanghai to you and me? Warlords waste no time seeking loot in fishing villages. Even should trouble come to the city near by—*we* need not starve. Still the sea will give us fish, and the ground, peanuts and sweet potatoes." He yawned, much to his grandson's annoyance. "Would that cabbages liked sand as well!"

"Old One, warlords are satisfied with loot; the Japanese are not. They would take this land for their own and make all Chinese slaves. At Shanghai, it is said, they kill villagers as well as the military. The officers at the Fort advise our neighbors to move inland."

"What did you say?" Lao To demanded, then hurried on, "I have lived too long to be frightened by such talk. When enemy ships come here, that day you and I may squeeze heart, not now."

"If they come also in flying-boats as the soldiers fear— what of that?"

Grandfather refused to continue the argument. He had already caught up a hoe and started toward the cabbage patch. San-djiu, the news still heavy on his mind, stood looking after the bent figure. What the Old One had said was true—there would be time enough to get away from ships. But if the danger came by air, that was something else again. While several small planes were now attached to the barrack's defense equipment, the enemy was supposed to have hundreds. It might be wiser, as some neighbors had already decided, to leave this dangerous location for a time. Where to go and how to persuade Grandfather to act against his will were the real problems. "*Muh iu fa tz!* (No help for it!)" Thirty-nine told himself, and, catching up a net, began to search for broken strands.

The next morning the first bombers came up on the horizon out of Japan.

CHAPTER II

"When the Typhoon Blows It Is Wise to Bend with the Gale"

SEEING the airplanes first against the backdrop of early morning sky, San-djiu let the anchor rope slide automatically to sea bottom, and squinted upward in bewilderment. These machines were unlike the planes at the Fort both in size and design, and the uncomfortable conviction that they belonged to the enemy was followed by the question of where they might be bound.

Approach was swift; while such a thing still seemed impossible, the bombers roared low over the fishing fleet. A moment later, they circled in formation above village and Fort, whirred again toward the boats, then began to climb.

Suddenly like some predatory bird pursuing its victim, the leading plane swooped. At the same moment a small object tore through the air, seemed to grow larger as it neared the boats, then plunged into the depths. Replacing this, a giant geyser shot up to link sea and sky, fell back, and, in turn, was succeeded by a series of mountainous waves surging shoreward.

The fishing crews, engrossed in watching the plane, now found themselves in dangerous straits. Thirty-nine's sampan leaped from one trough to another, and the boy, expecting each minute to be washed overboard, clung desperately to the cabin's arched bamboo framework. When the sea eventually quieted, he had only one idea—to reach land and discover his grandfather's fate. Without stopping to gather the dead fish floating everywhere on the surface, he poled straightway to shore.

Standing at the door of the hut with a puzzled frown on his face, Lao To called out, "Did the water buffalo that holds the earth stretch?"

Thirty-nine breathed deeply in relief. "So you are all right, Old One! No, that was no earthquake—a Japanese flying machine threw a bomb."

Grandfather stared. "A bomb?" he repeated questioningly.

"You have forgotten what I told you. Our enemy puts gunpowder into steel things, then drops them to earth."

"Why?"

"To destroy buildings and people. I think that was meant for the Fort, not the sea. *Ai!*" prompted by memory he interrupted himself. "I must go back—good fish are to be had in plenty." Turning, he ran down the hill.

"No need is there for haste," a passing fisherman told him, halting to point toward his own heaped buckets. "Hundreds have washed in on the sand; were they even one-tenth alive, we might all become rich."

"Truly!" Thirty-nine agreed, aware that neither Fort nor city market would purchase dead fish, however fresh. He turned to call over his shoulder, "That was a bomb—not so?"

The other nodded. "What else? Though they must have plenty, to waste them in water. Old Tang's boat turned over, but his friend, Wu, rescued him."

During the rest of that day, while the villagers busied themselves cooking or salting fish for future home use, they talked of nothing but the recent experience. If a bomb falling to sea bottom could kill fish in this fashion, what then might one do to men who lacked even watery depths in which to hide, they asked themselves and found no answer.

Near dusk San-djiu, impelled by curiosity about the military's reaction to this matter made his way up the white, sandy road to the Fort. A familiar sentry firmly halted him at the entrance. "Is this the hour to sell things, Worthless One?" he demanded.

"Truly, a little late," replied Thirty-nine, "but I would speak with the cook. I have some fine salted fish for him," he added, extending a basket for the other man to consider.

"Tonight he has no use for them; everybody from this building digs a place of safety underground. Now go home! It is my business to watch the sky, not to talk with villagers."

A little later, sitting on the narrow bench before the hut, San-djiu asked his grandfather, "Old One, if the Japanese soon return, what then?"

"In the morning after a night's sleep, I will talk over this affair. Until then we can lay down our hearts," Lao To declared and rising, went within.

As he had so often done before, the youth remained to gaze in the direction of the Fort. The white rays of moonlight outlined barrack and village almost as clearly as did the noonday sun. The unhappy thought came that this enemy would pay little attention to what Grandfather considered proper hours for fighting wars. With a target so clearly to be seen, was there any reason why they should not return tonight and ruin the lonely gray stone building that had meant so much in his life? And in that case, what of these homes about him? Many villages around Shanghai had been destroyed. Was it likely this one would escape? How many people could a bomb kill? And who might they be? A chill ran up his back. At the Fort men were digging a place of refuge underground, and while the neighbors would think such a precaution foolish, he would nevertheless mention it tomorrow. If only Lao To were safe inland, his own mind would be relieved of its greatest concern.

During the night, Thirty-nine tossed restlessly, struggling in a dream of deep-sea monsters that threatened to engulf his sampan and himself time after time. To and fro he pitched as the small craft fell from one wave crest to another. Suddenly the boat went from under him and his body was caught in snapping jaws and dragged to the depths. Trying ineffectually to scream, he woke only to find himself half buried beneath loose earth.

A roaring in his head deafened him to all other sounds, and as yet unable to escape nightmare's clutch, the youth believed himself miraculously rescued from drowning and washed up on the sands. For several moments he lay inert, grateful at being still alive. Then consciousness of some worry outside himself stirred his mind awake. Opening eyes experimentally, he soon became aware that this present resting place was not on the shore but in the village street. What then had happened to him and where was Lao To? Freeing an arm, he began feverishly to dig at his earthy shroud.

Unharmed save for surface wounds and temporary deafness, San-djiu managed to liberate himself and stand erect in what might have been the setting for some Taoist Hell. In the distance the Fort was a mass of flames. Above it the reflecting sky, discolored like the tissues about an angry wound, glowed in blackened red. In sharp contrast the cloudy film of settling sand, straw, and plaster that curtained the Point turned to pearl beneath the touch of Dawn's exploring fingers.

What the growing light revealed made Thirty-nine sway with faintness. Figures ominously quiet stretched full length in slowly widening pools of blood. An extended hand separated from its original owner still seemed to reach for help, and a torso without limbs sat propped in grotesque fashion against a crazily tilting wall. Like ants laboring to restore a demolished hill, the uninjured villagers, crawling back frantically over the flimsy bridge between Death and Life, now began the desperate work of search and salvage. The faces of all were twisted with anguish, and their lips mouthing tortured cries seemed to the deafened youth a soundless horror accenting all others. He took a step forward and stumbled over the dead body of Old Tang, rescued ironically by Wu from drowning the day before. Hysteria clutched at San-djiu's mind. Turning aside he retched violently. Then bringing this spasm of revulsion under control, he looked about for Lao To and what once had been their home.

That Old Head was still alive seemed unlikely. When the youth came upon the old man sitting in their own familiar vegetable patch half hidden beneath a mat of loosened roof thatch, his relief knew no bounds. "Grandfather! Grandfather!" he cried out. There was no answer. *Ai-ya*, perhaps his ears are bad like mine! he told himself, running hands swiftly over the other in search of injury.

Without recognition the elder continued to stare at his grandson, who now half pulled, half lifted the aged figure to a small, unencumbered strip of earth and set it gently down. Lao To accepted these moves with docility, sitting as still as any wooden toy exactly where he had been placed. For a moment or two Thirty-nine experienced panic, then shouldering this newest responsibility, began to plan. Something had happened to the Old One's head and, until recovery occurred, his grandson would have to make all decisions.

Since the youth was unable to guess at the enemy's purpose for this devastated spot, escape seemed most urgent of all needs. One swift glance had already shown him the sampan riding securely in the inlet. The immediate task

"Grandfather! Grandfather!" he cried out.

was to collect whatever necessities could be found among the ruins of their home, then loading these and Grandfather aboard the boat, seek refuge somewhere by sea.

Three walls of the hut were gone; one still provided a recognizable landmark. The furniture was in splinters; *pu-gai* (comforts stuffed with cotton wadding), though torn and smeared with dirt, could still be used. From the mass of wreckage he extricated two battered iron cooking pots and one badly chipped bowl, the only remaining dish. To his great dismay, Grandfather's pipe and tobacco as well as the buckets containing their day's water supply had disappeared completely. With the community well buried beneath débris, water suddenly became the chief problem. Kept aboard the boat was a covered bucketful and this, if still intact (for he had no idea how much the sampan might have been jarred in the night's explosions), would be enough for temporary use, at least. He had been fortunate in finding their tin of cheap tea crushed flat but still unopened; and in a mound of freshly thrown earth, scattered grains of rice and dried peas were to be seen.

When these last had been salvaged, he lifted as many objects as could be carried at one time, glanced worriedly at his grandfather who had shown no sign of voluntary action, then started downhill to the sampan. The water supply there, Kuan-yin (Goddess of Mercy) be praised! was as he had left it. With the portable charcoal stove kept on board for all-day journeys, the question of immediate food and its preparation was settled. On the second trip he caught up the remaining articles, and coaxing Lao To to his feet, led the old man down the hill to the boat. Aboard he placed the other comfortably on *pu-gai*, stored the meager supplies, hauled in the anchor, and pulled away from shore.

The crumbling Fort was now lost to the eye in billows of smoke, and he wondered bleakly about the fate of its inmates. Not a single soldier had come to help the stricken villagers, nor had the fishermen concerned themselves about saving the barracks from flame. He, himself, with an attachment to the building much stronger than that of most people, had in the midst of disaster given it little thought. With a start he realized that his mind had been so intent on escape that he had not even tried to hold speech with any of his neighbors. What Grandfather had always insisted seemed painfully true—in time of trouble, each family had to fight for itself.

This morning the sea was smooth, its surface broken only by the familiar running of waves on sand. It seemed beyond belief that the sky, peaceful with fleecy clouds, could ever have harbored steel vultures that dropped eggs of destruction on helpless people. Shaking with chill, Thirty-nine wondered if the years to come would ever release him from the memory of the horrors he had just witnessed.

Through long centuries of disaster, it had been Chinese custom to build anew on ruins. Always the men and women of his race clung doggedly to familiar bits of soil, their only stable possession in a terrifyingly unstable world. This was what Lao To, still in authority, would have done; and for the first time in life his grandson, suspecting the elder's probable wishes, was deliberately refusing to consider them. Perhaps he, Li San-djiu-tz, lacked the stubbornness of his ancestors, his mind suggested. Given assurance that enemy bombers would never again attack the Point, he still did not want to remain there where all that had lent boyhood meaning was now ruthlessly destroyed.

It was true that deep beneath everything else had been his dream of one day seeking fortune in some city where wealth and adventure had become traditional. He had hoped to start out as a man grown and with a little carefully hoarded silver jingling in his moneybag. Instead he was leaving home at fifteen, responsible for two people and almost destitute. Well, it was not the way of Life to let men say when and where they would meet Fortune or, having met her, whether she would be good or bad. He and Lao To were still both alive, and with sampan and nets they would not soon starve. Burdened with mud, grime, and weariness, his bare young shoulders seemed slighter than usual, as he poled with steady, unerring strokes toward open sea.

CHAPTER III

*"If You Dare Not Enter the Tiger's Den, How Can You Hope
to Capture Its Cub?"*

O N THE far side of the Point the shore line, rocky in
formation, rose steeply from the sea. In that direction
San-djiu headed. Familiarity with this particular stretch of
coast and its possibilities as a refuge, had influenced his first
decision to flee by water. On several occasions in the past,
hoping for mild adventure, he had explored the section and
found it very different from the broad, sandy beach of his
own inlet.

Centuries of pounding surf had cut caverns of varying
depths into the rock. In late years, however, only the worst

23

typhoons had lifted waves to the higher recesses and, as a result, sea birds flocked to them for shelter. At the moment such a location seemed to offer greater safety from falling bombs than any other close by, and until more definite plans could be made for the future, this place would do.

The first problem was to find a landing place where the sampan would not be broken up by changing tides. With this accomplished, Thirty-nine scrambled over slanting shale toward the largest of the higher caves. As he stooped beneath an overhanging shelf of rock at the entrance, a rush of wings beat about his head and several angry gulls flew past him into the sunlight.

Their dung was thick on the stony floor, and he began at once to stack this accumulation of filth in a corner for fuel. That the place stank and harbored an army of lice worried the new tenant very little. The poor of his race learned early to accustom themselves to unpleasantnesses, and neither he nor his grandfather would complain of minor discomforts. When the place was finally settled to his satisfaction and Lao To installed within, Thirty-nine brewed tea. After a steaming bowl, the old man stretched out again on his comforts and instantly returned to slumber.

Drowsing wearily over his own portion, the youth tried to plan for the future. His most urgent need was fresh water; already a fourth of their supply had been used for tea and the rice now steaming on the charcoal stove. Fish, of course, were to be had in plenty; also, while the birds had left no eggs in this cave, there would doubtless be some in the neighboring ones.

His ears were clearing rapidly, for he could now hear the shrill-crying gulls and the deeper roar of the surf. How long Old Head would continue like this was the greatest problem. Overcome suddenly by exhaustion the grandson also lay down and went to sleep.

A pungent odor of scorching rice disturbed his rest. After rescuing the food and assuring himself that Lao To would not soon wake, San-djiu slipped outside to explore the neighborhood. A half hour's thorough searching provided him with five eggs. With these safely in hand, he paused on the edge of a cliff to wonder where in this lonely world of rocks and sea and plaintive, wheeling birds, a fresh-water spring might be found. The unexpected sound of his own name startled him out of this discouraged mood, and he turned sharply to recognize Ding, an old soldier of long years' acquaintance.

"*Ai!* Where did you come from?" Thirty-nine demanded, hurrying forward, then became silent as one of the Fort lieutenants abruptly joined them.

Ding eased the meeting by a word or two, and the officer asked, "What is your business here?"

"This morning, Honorable Sir, my grandfather and I sought shelter among these rocks. He is ill."

"Injured?"

"Inside his head. No longer can he recognize me."

"The great noise does that to many men."

"Soon he will be better, not so?"

"Perhaps! Others have recovered. Now a few questions I would ask you: first, have you food?"

"Enough, but little water."

"Good!" said the Lieutenant. "Ding knows of a spring halfway between here and the Fort. We shall exchange water for food."

Mention of the barracks prompted the youth to inquire, "Sir, those others—what happened to them?"

"Many died, our captain among them. The rest now help villagers who wish to enter the city."

So soldiers and civilians *were* working together, Thirty-nine reminded himself with a surge of comfort. But why were these two not with the others?

As if answering the unspoken question, the officer continued, "Young Li, when Ding saw you, he said it was good fortune, since you can be trusted. That is important. Soon the enemy's ships will come on the sea. When they do, you also may serve your country."

"Most unworthy!" murmured Thirty-nine, puzzled and disturbed.

"Hidden here, Ding and I hope to learn what may be of use to the officer in command of city troops. On arrival, the Japanese will land men to guard the Point and the road to the city." The Lieutenant eyed him gravely then added, "While no soldier could hope to slip past them with a message, a clever fisherman might."

For a moment San-djiu made no reply to this suggestion. The thought of going near the devastated village and Fort seemed almost as terrible as meeting the enemy soldiers, should they come as this officer seemed to expect. "If I fail —who would care for Grandfather?" he asked slowly.

"A fair question, but I cannot answer it. In war a soldier uses every means for his country's defense. You, not I, must say whether you will help."

With each sentence Thirty-nine felt older. A fishing-boy, accustomed to obeying his elder's commands, he was now being treated as an equal by this army officer, an unusual experience indeed. But even the sweetest peach had a bitter stone, he thought with a sigh, recognizing that the new respect carried with it an equally new responsibility. That millions of China's young were likewise soon to be tested on the question of first loyalties was beyond his knowledge. Lao To's generation would, by custom and tradition, have found only one answer in deciding between family and country. A man's supreme duty, so the ancestors had taught, lay with those under his roof; preserving the government was the task of rulers and officials. Conscripted against their will for military duty, ordinary citizens went bitterly; fighting, they believed, was soldiers' work—artisans and farmers could find better use for their strength.

Yet he, San-djiu-tz, was being asked to decide between Old Head, who was his whole family, and the Central Government at Nanking. In those days of patriotic enthusiasm before the bombing—he paused aghast at the realization that the bombing had happened only a few hours ago—most villagers had echoed glibly the current phrases. But to him at this moment, "Nationalist Government" and "Chiang Kai-shek" were still just phrases and little more. Was he for a few empty words to risk leaving Grandfather uncared for and unprotected? The very idea was absurd. On the other

hand, Common Sense reminded him, if this implacable enemy
were offered no opposition, how long could Lao To, and himself for that matter, expect to remain alive?

Even as attention darted painfully from one argument to
the other, some corner of his mind was considering ways of
carrying the message past the sentries into town. A villager,
the officer had suggested, might do what soldiers could not.
It was said that the "dwarfs" lived on fish—and a fisherman
selling his catch might—*ai!*

Lifting his eyes to the officer whose gaze had never left
him, he was astonished to hear his own voice say slowly, "If
their ships come, Sir, I will think up a plan. Now I must go
to Lao To."

"Not too fast!" interrupted Ding. "The food you would
exchange for water—what of that?"

"First a look at Old Head, then I will cast a net. But the
water—how will you carry it without buckets?"

"Lay down your heart, that is my worry," the soldier
replied.

For three days the refugees in the caves shared resources
and worked to increase supplies. Using a foreign pencil
and scraps of rice paper, the officer spent long hours sketch-
ing the rocky coast line. At other times while his companions foraged for supplies, he kept close watch over the old
man who lay so helplessly lost in sleep.

Thirty-nine fished, collected bird eggs, and searched for
shellfish between changing tides. Since it was highly important that water other than that for immediate use be stored
for emergency, Ding made two trips inland daily. There he

usually found some sort of container in which to bring back
the supply, and often he had a bit of green vegetable as well.

His reports of these excursions afforded sad but interesting conversation at the evening meal. Naturally enough, he
made few references to the deserted fort, now a mass of
charred ruins, but talked rather freely about the village.
Five or six fishing families, he related, had refused to seek
safety in the city and were already rebuilding from the wreckage. These were so absorbed in their tasks that they paid
scant attention to his frequent arrivals in their midst.

One evening Ding's booty consisted of three large cabbages
and several sweet potatoes.

"*Ai!* Where did you find so much?" San-djiu wanted to
know.

"I think from your own garden. Your home was nearest
the Point, *hsi puh hsi?* (Yes, not yes?)"

The youth nodded. "There were no more?"

Ding spread his lower lip. "Would I have left them for
others?"

Thirty-nine was silent; he was remembering the long,
weary hours that Old Head and he had spent tilling the soil.
And here before him was the harvest. For a long time that
night the grandson lay awake wondering about the future.
Provided the enemy stayed away, this cave with a matting
square at the entrance to keep out the worst winter storms
and a small stock of charcoal for fuel when bird dung and
driftwood were not to be procured, would furnish a satisfactory shelter. As always their food would be largely fish.
Rice and green vegetables could be purchased when he sold his

catch in the city, which would now be his only market, provided, he repeated, that the Japanese stayed away. Should they come by ship, it was possible they too might buy from him; on the other hand they might . . . ! Shivering, he left this thought unfinished and soon fell into restless sleep.

When he awoke at the usual early hour, a dense fog shrouded the cliffs and did nothing to lighten his spirits. Satisfied after routine chores as to Lao To's comfort, he waited under the overhanging rock at the entrance for Ding to arrive and stay with the old man. Following this, the youth picked his steps cautiously down to where the sampan was moored, cast off, and began poling slowly, unable to see a foot ahead through the wall of mist. With a sudden decision not to tempt Fortune too much by blind venturing, he reached for the anchor and was startled into frozen attention by the slap-slap of feet on a deck, together with the sound of voices in an unfamiliar tongue.

Much as if his staring eyes had bored a hole in the fog, a small, jagged opening gradually appeared and in it was dimly outlined the stern of a great vessel only a few yards away. In a second or two fog again shuttered this artificial window, and Thirty-nine, shaking from head to foot over his discovery, made for home. "Ding!" he called in a harsh whisper, as he clambered from shore to cave. "Ding, hurry a little! A ship has come and is anchored just below!"

To his surprise the Lieutenant appeared at once beside the other and demanded, "One or more?"

"Sir, I do not know. I saw only one but it was great in size."

In the fog . . . was dimly outlined the stern of a great vessel.

"They saw you?"

"No, I am nine-tenths certain."

"Good! Though they will soon discover your boat and search for its owner. That we may not bring harm to you and Old Head, Ding and I will leave before the fog disappears." He paused, then continued, "You are not too stupid a fisherman, but you must pretend to be so, when they come."

San-djiu nodded, then asked, "Where will you go, Honorable Sir, and how will you learn what you wish to know?"

The officer gestured toward fields beyond the cliff. "Over there. As to the enemy—you must be our eyes in this place, while we watch their landing parties farther inland. Before they place guards at the city gate, Ding will carry a message inside. Tonight I myself will return here to talk with you." He paused, frowning. "First, do you recognize warships?"

"They are dark gray, yes, not yes?"

"Right, and the merchantmen, black. To be ten-tenths certain—the battleships have a white flag with a rising sun in the center; the others, white with a red ball. Three other things are important: what is on their decks, how deeply they set in the water, and whether the soldiers are many or few."

The youth scratched his head. "Why is this?"

"That I may learn what kind of equipment is carried and how much—heavy artillery or just men, small arms, and food." For a moment the speaker seemed lost in thought, then hastily writing characters on a scrap of paper, he placed this in Thirty-nine's hand and said slowly, "Wait—listen carefully! If I do not return here by dawn, you must find a way into the city before the sun is high in the sky. Follow the street of the West Gate to the Confucian Temple. Three doors beyond that is a raw-silk shop. There ask for the proprietor, Giao, give him this paper, and tell him all that you have seen. Should he be away, then wait for him; do not talk with anyone else—their spies are everywhere!"

San-djiu repeated carefully, "West Gate Road, raw-silk shop three doors past Confucian Temple—ask for Giao." Suddenly his eyes narrowed. "Sir, if not tonight, when will you come?"

Exchanging a swift glance with Ding, the Lieutenant replied, "After tonight, do not expect me." Abruptly he changed the subject. "Remember one thing only, Young Li, the lives of many people may depend on this message to Giao!" A smile lightened his grave expression. "May you and your grandfather again know peace! Now give us some cooked food and that tin of boiling water!"

Ding, always of few words, murmured a brief farewell as he caught up these supplies, and in another moment the two soldiers had disappeared into the shrouding mist.

Divided between relief over their departure from the cliffs and fear of what the immediate future might bring to Lao To and himself, the youth stood staring at the scrap of paper in his hand. A sudden spurt of curiosity made him wonder what it said. Most fishermen could neither read nor write, and until this moment he himself had known no desire to do so. It was not likely, though, that he would ever do books. That took money, of which he had none, as well as brains—and while he was not exactly an empty-head, he was also not a scholar, of that much his mind was sure.

The paper, he decided, must be hidden at once and in some place where the "dwarfs" would not be likely to look should they discover this cave. Calculatingly he glanced about him, then placed the written message with his supply of uncooked provisions in a closed container. This he carried to another cave to bury beneath a pile of refuse.

Returning, he put more water on to boil, brewed tea, pulled the old man awake long enough to drink and eat of the remaining prepared food, then smothered the firepot with ashes. There was a possibility that the Japanese sailors would not notice the sampan in its quiet cove behind jutting rocks, and he had no intention of attracting them here by either the sight or smell of smoke. Next, with his own stomach filled, he sat down in the shadow of the doorway and stared toward the sea.

For what seemed an interminable length of time the fog continued. Inactivity and the blanketing moisture made him sleepy; only the Lieutenant's statement that lives might depend on what he learned kept him from dozing. He wondered where the two soldiers had found a hiding place. While his own predicament was highly dangerous, theirs in Chinese army uniforms were much more so for they would probably be killed on sight. At this moment the full meaning of the order, "If I do not come tonight, do not expect me!" swept over him. Failure to return would tell him without words that the Lieutenant had been captured or killed.

More than once through the years he had heard Old Head quote to fishermen afraid of threatening seas, " 'If you dare not enter the tiger's den, how can you hope to capture its cub?' "

He sucked in his breath sharply, realizing for the first time that all the talk about men serving their country had not been empty sounds. Knowing that they risked torture and death, both officer and private had chosen to remain in this dangerous neighborhood instead of escaping into the city before the Nipponese landed. What was more, they had made this choice freely and for one reason only—that their information about the enemy might be complete. In promising to help outwit the aggressors, he, too, had agreed to risk much, but by so doing he would become one of a great brotherhood.

As if to bolster his resolution, light began to penetrate the mist and a broken strip of blue appeared above him. In another moment three great ships came into view on the water below. Motionless as a bronze Buddha in a shrine, Li Thirty-nine squatted at the entrance to the cave and waited for what next might happen.

CHAPTER IV

So This Is My Enemy!

ALTHOUGH only one of the three vessels was dark gray, all flew the naval ensign. The warship, of deeper draught than the others, apparently carried the bulk of equipment, for the decks of the transformed merchantmen were thick with men. Aside from these simple facts, Thirty-nine's limited knowledge prevented his discovering more of interest to the Lieutenant. His attention now centered on the men themselves. As he watched, a number of them dropped over the sides of the transports into small boats and made for shore. From the cruiser two motor launches put out, and the staccato sound of engines seemed to add rhythm to the whole procedure. That the Japanese did not expect defensive ac-

36

tion from the Chinese seemed clear, for no precautions were used to keep their movements secret.

It was not until the invaders began scrambling up the cliffs that San-djiu became fully aware of his own predicament. Why was he, alone, waiting here while this powerful enemy approached? As if in direct answer to the question, some protective instinct forced him to his feet. He left the cave and, hugging the shadowed rocks with the craftiness of a hunted animal, began to clamber toward the heights. Once there on level ground, it would be easy to cross fields and seek refuge behind the city wall.

For the moment, Fear chained him to the single-minded purpose of escaping. The past with its record of personal courage, filial devotion, and recently developed patriotism might never have existed. Only as he pulled himself up on the plateau, did the familiar sense of responsibility make itself felt. Like the faintly disturbing whir of some distant watchman's rattle in the night, the words, "Lao To, Lao To, Lao To," began to sound. "Lao To sick and helpless— Lao To left to meet the barbarians alone!"

Thirty-nine shook his head in a physical effort to rid himself of these nagging thoughts. Surely not even the East-Ocean "dwarfs" would harm the aged, Fear argued sullenly —not even they could be that evil. Torn by indecision, the youth faltered, then stood still, staring across the fields toward the city and the safety that seemed to dwell within its walls. After a long moment he turned about, and slowly retracing the way to the cave, entered and knelt beside the quiet figure on the bedding.

Lost in some happier existence, Old Head, his face peaceful and serene, lay unchanged, oblivious to the worries and problems of other men. "Grandfather, Grandfather," Thirty-nine whispered unhappily. Then gently tucking the *pu-gai* about the other's thin shoulders, he got to his feet and resumed his vigil at the entrance.

For some time no more landing parties appeared. The ships, however, seemed alive with activity, although what this was the distant watcher could only guess. By mid-afternoon groups of scouts in twos and threes returned. There was something ludicrous about the way in which their short-legged, stocky bodies moved over the rocks, and for a moment San-djiu forgot everything else in the fascination of studying their progress. No wonder that his own people, whose movements were so different, called these others "dwarfs," he told himself.

The reappearance of the scouts must have been the signal for action on board the vessels. More boatloads of men and equipment were now lowered and started ashore. During the rest of the afternoon soldiers and carriers filed upward in the direction of ruined fort and village. The youth wondered uneasily about the families Ding had said remained on the Point.

For Lao To and himself the threat of danger seemed to decrease with every minute. Soon the sun would set, and from experience he knew that in his native skies darkness would follow at once. After nightfall the Lieutenant might arrive any time and thereby put an end to Li Thirty-nine's responsibility for delivering the message.

Lost in these comforting hopes, he was startled almost out of his wits by a kick that sent him sprawling. He rose to face three Japanese, one of whom instantly pinned him against the wall with outthrust bayonet, then burst into unintelligible speech. The second entered the cave and the last, whose uniform indicated an officer's rank, stood by silently taking in the scene.

The Lieutenant's advice to feign stupidity under such circumstances had been unnecessary. Breathless from shock, terrified by the weapon pricking his bare body, and unable to understand a word that his captor had said, Thirty-nine could not have seemed anything else. Suddenly their leader stepped forward and, waving aside his subordinate, interrupted in labored Chinese, "Who are you? Why are you here?"

This garbled speech sounded almost as strange as Nipponese to the frightened victim's ears, but after a puzzled moment he managed to stammer out answers.

"Say that again!" came the order.

San-djiu obeyed, this time speaking more slowly. To his relief the third soldier, having swiftly looked over the cave, now came out. In their own language the three of them talked volubly, their words coming peculiarly through narrowed, half closed lips.

Soon the officer resumed questioning, "The old man— who is he?"

"My grandfather."

"Where are the others?"

"Have none."

"Hard to believe!"

"It is true."

"How long have you lived here?"

For a second the youth felt it might be wise to answer "always," thus avoiding mention of the destroyed village, a dangerous subject at best. Such a reply, however, carried its own risk; some villager questioned later about him and Old Head might, innocently enough, reveal the facts. Instead he told the real story briefly, repeating even the simplest phrases twice in order to make the Japanese understand.

"That is your sampan below, is it not?"

Thirty-nine nodded. So they had already found his boat!

"How many fish do you catch?"

An average haul was mentioned.

"You sell them?"

"At the—the city," San-djiu answered, hastily swallowing the word "Fort."

Unnoticing, the officer continued, "In the future you, like those others, may remain here to fish, but you will bring the whole catch to us."

The whole catch, he repeated to himself. What then do *we* eat? Resentment now pushed fear aside. This evil thing does not mean to pay me for my fish—that is certain —and without money, how buy other food? If only he dared to ask them that! Instead, his lips managed to say, "Where shall I carry the fish?"

"To the ships. I will tell our men so they do not shoot you. Thus we will save both bullets and fish." The Japanese sucked in his breath. "The more you bring, the better for you! Try no tricks, Chinese Dog, or you will wish we had *shot* you."

The next minute they were gone. Trembling uncontrollably, San-djiu stared after them, then spat where they had stood. He was torn between terror and anger. That they had kicked him and called him, "Chinese Dog," was bitter to the taste, but he had been cursed and knocked about so often by soldiers at the Fort that such treatment could be endured when necessary. What did enrage him was that these rotten eggs would force Chinese to spend strength for them without pay. "You, like those others," they had said, and meant doubtless the fishermen still on the Point. In his land poor men labored from dawn to dark but they did so for themselves and their families. Even boy apprentices learning trades were given food and shelter in return; also, most of these dwelt in cities where people were known to put up with things no countryman would stand. Yet he and several others from his village had suddenly become slaves to the despised East-Ocean men. *"Ai-ya!"* he exclaimed bitterly, then turned and slowly entered the cave.

As usual now, Old Head had been undisturbed by what went on about him. For a moment his grandson knew a deep, unhappy longing for the other's companionship and advice. Perhaps some hot food might be good for both of them, and since this refuge had already been discovered, there was no reason why the charcoal ashes should not be blown to flame.

After the meal the coals were once more smothered so their glow might add no hazard to the Lieutenant's arrival. Then wrapping himself in the torn *pu-gai*, Thirty-nine leaned back against the wall to wait. Somber clouds shadowed the moon foretelling bad weather on the morrow. From this location the ships riding at anchor without lights and veiled by the mist that rose along the shore line, bulked in vague, sinister shapes. They brought to mind ugly, unfamiliar creatures of the depths that occasionally appeared in fishermen's nets and for a brief time made all who saw them think with dread of the waters from which the community won its living. There below him in the night floated three man-made monsters of the Eastern Sea with a power to harm his people far greater than that of any living creature, however horrible.

It came to him suddenly that until today he had met the enemy only in the words of other men, much like characters in a shadow play once seen at New Year's in the city. The tales of cruelty at Shanghai had stirred him, but not deeply —Shanghai was a long journey from the village on the Point. Even when bombs had destroyed his home and injured Lao To, the evil had seemed somehow to come from Heaven rather than from human beings. He had called the Japanese, as did all his neighbors, "devils" and "dwarfs," but there had been nothing personal about any of these terms. They were simply invaders who must be driven from China's soil, and little more.

Those few moments of personal contact, however, had changed his feeling. Kicked and cursed and threatened with death from a bayonet, he had shaken with terror, and these experiences were not soon to be forgotten. But what really stuck in his throat was the knowledge that he was their prisoner and from now on must do only what they commanded. Neither he nor Old Head would starve for a few days at least. There was still the hidden food, and it would not be too difficult to steal and cook an occasional fish between the casting of nets. But to call those barbarians "Master"—*ai*! Dimly he was beginning to understand what the Government meant by the term "National Freedom."

From infancy he had been taught to respect the family name, Li, so that his conduct might never bring disgrace on the ancestors. At present in Japanese hands, he burned with a sense of racial pride far beyond anything previously felt even when Chiang Kai-shek's officers at the Fort had talked so hotly of patriotism. Today, as if by magic the shadow-players had become real men, and China's enemies his personal foes.

Darkness and the monotonous roar of the surf made him sleepy, and Time crept through the night with feeble steps. As it progressed he felt increasingly hopeless about the Lieutenant's return. With the invaders in full possession of this section, it would be foolish indeed for the other to make such an attempt. And that meant that he, Li San-djiu-tz, would have to deliver the message to Giao. But how?

His original plan, when first made, had seemed very clever, indeed. Supposedly the Japanese soldiers would be stationed on the road to the city; there he would carry the fish and offer them for sale. Since his only garment, blue cotton trousers, might be searched, any message—in this case the Lieutenant's note to Giao—must be hidden in a dead fish. The soldiers would, of course, throw the bad fish at him. Tossing it back into the bucket, he would ask permission to go buy a small measure of rice and would slip within the city gate.

Now with no fish to sell, and his movements limited to sea and ships, there would not be a chance of setting foot on the road. Moreover, the city authorities certainly must have had some word of the Japanese landing this afternoon. With such knowledge would they fail to barricade the gate? He had been *ben deh hun* (stupid, indeed) not to think of these things before.

From the appearance of the stormy sky it was difficult to judge the hour, but the night must be two thirds gone. By this time the Lieutenant was probably dead. The thought made the youth shiver and pull the bedding more tightly about him. His mouth stretched in a succession of yawns, and drowsiness temporarily shut out the world.

A sound that belonged neither to sea nor wind pulled him abruptly awake. With every sense alert he strained to listen, but made no other move. Should this be the Lieutenant, nothing must be done to attract attention here; on the other hand, if an enemy spy came, that one should find only a grandfather and grandson innocently slumbering. Since there was no animal life on the cliffs and the birds were quiet, the sound, coming always nearer, belonged to human feet—of that he was certain. Then a moving shadow, darker even than the shades of night, sidled into the cave and after a cautious moment whispered, "Li, it is I."

San-djiu drew a relieved breath. "Truly, Sir, your daring is great!" he murmured in admiration. "How did you escape them?"

"That is a long tale," replied the other, sitting on the floor.

"Do they follow?"

"Not now. There was a sentry near where I lay hidden. Before he could call out, I killed him."

"You did not shoot the gun—how then?"

"My hands about his throat." The officer sighed wearily. "Kuan-yin have mercy! I am tired!"

Thirty-nine's flesh crawled. This man beside him had just killed another—*Ai-ya* what a business! "You wish food?" he asked, suddenly anxious to change the subject. "I smothered the fire but the water kettle on the ashes is still warm."

"Good!"

The youth rose, moved to the entrance, and listened carefully. Then he poured out a bowl of warm water and handed this with the pan of food to the other.

"Now, while I eat, tell me all that has happened," ordered the Lieutenant.

Afterwards he said, "That you fish for them is good fortune!"

San-djiu's jaw sagged. "Good fortune? I do not understand."

"Listen a little! I have a new plan. There is a space beneath your boat deck large enough to hide me. When you go to fish, I shall be aboard and thus learn all I need to know. Before you bring in the catch, you can set me ashore at some safer place up the coast, and I will return overland to the city's North Gate."

"Suppose they discover you on the boat, Sir, then they will kill the three of us."

"*Muh iu fa tz!* (There is no help for it!) We must risk that, though I promise you it is not my meaning to be caught."

Thirty-nine remained silent. His mind was busy with a plan of its own. He said slowly, "I too will go ashore up the coast. There is a village with a Confucian Temple six or seven *li* (three *li* make a mile) from here. Twice I have been there with Grandfather."

"This time—what of the Old One?"

"He goes with us. I will not leave him here alone; moreover, I shall not come back."

It was the officer's turn to be silent. This move would increase the danger, yet he could understand Young Li's feeling about Lao To. Finally he inquired, "How will you carry him to the boat?"

"Leaning on my strength, he climbed here; to go down will be easier."

"And if some sentry on the shore does not permit your grandfather to leave?"

"Then I must think up a better way," the youth persisted stubbornly.

"At that other village what will you do?"

"Who can read the future? One thing only I know— I cannot stay here to help these East-Ocean 'devils' destroy our land."

"Very well! Now before light comes, I must hide in the boat. Would that you had a garment to lend me! I might pass for a fisherman."

"And if you meet a Japanese?"

"It is my business not to meet one. As for you—do not be too slow in coming to fish. Beneath your deck there will be little room for my arms and legs."

"There will also be some water," Thirty-nine informed him.

"Ugh!" grunted the other, then with the utmost caution, he disappeared again into the night.

CHAPTER V

"To Dig Up a Tree, Begin at the Root"

THIRTY-NINE lifted the kettle of warm water and drank from the spout. Weary though he was, all thought of sleep had fled, for there was much to be done between now and daylight. He hoped the signs of bad weather meant a fog, at least while the boat was being loaded.

The first thing now was to destroy the note to Giao. Making his way carefully toward the other cave, he rescued the hidden food tin, took out the scrap of paper, and proceeded to chew it up, spitting the sodden bits into the heaps of bird dung.

Back in his own place, the youth tried to decide whether Lao To or their belongings should be carried first to the boat. If only everything might be done in one trip! To help his grandfather down seemed most important; then if anything happened to cut off his own return here, the two of them would at least be together, although without bedding, stove, or food.

The Hour of the Tiger (3:00 A.M. to 5:00 A.M.) must be halfway gone, for the darkness seemed to be losing depth. They must wait until dawn at least. The enemy would certainly not permit him to start out while night lasted. Also, though he himself could crawl over the cliffs like a cat, Lao To could not, and the grandson would need to watch where the old man was placing each unsteady footstep. Meanwhile they would eat heartily, for there was no way of knowing when the next meal might occur.

After their stomachs were filled, Thirty-nine tore several small squares of material from the ragged *pu-gai* and in these tied various items of food. His blue cotton pants were now rolled and twisted tightly above the knees; two or three of the foodstuff packets were placed in the bloused folds and the remaining ones were hidden in Old Head's garments. In the dark work had been slow indeed, and by the time these tasks were finished, dawn with the hoped-for fog had arrived.

Since the duration of such weather could never be counted on, no further time must be wasted. Within a few moments, the grandson had led his elder from the cave. Days of lying asleep had sapped Lao To's strength, and after each few steps he had to sit down. Fortunately the fog held and no one challenged their snail-like progress. Even the

shore of the little cove where his boat was anchored seemed
deserted, although the noise of activity aboard the vessels
came to them through the constant booming of the surf.
With great effort San-djiu got the old man aboard and set
him on the floor beneath the curved matting roof. After
secreting the food packets, he leaned toward the compart-
ment below and whispered, "Are you all right, Sir?"

"*Ko ee!* (Can do)" came the hushed reply. "You met
no one, yes or no?"

"No one. Now I go to bring the fire-basin and bedding."

"Hurry! I begin to feel like a frog."

Without further delay, Thirty-nine disappeared like a
wraith into the fog. His second trip was also uneventful and
at once the old man was made comfortable on the bedding.
The stove would attract no suspicion; most fishing boats
had them. Left behind in the cave were kettles, bowl, and
stored foodstuffs. The only real lack, though, was water
and this, since a third trip seemed a foolish challenge to
Good Fortune, would have to be borne until the new destination was reached.

For a fisherman to venture forth in such fog was a questionable move San-djiu fully recognized. However, with so
dangerous a cargo aboard, he felt impelled to haul in the
anchor and leave shore. As he reached for the poling oar,
his worst fear became reality. A figure loomed up suddenly
on the sandy beach and shouted in Japanese.

With thudding heart, the youth stared at the soldier.
Where had this sentry come from, and how long had he
been there hidden by the fog? Had he heard the hushed

Days of lying asleep had sapped Lao To's strength.

conversations with the Lieutenant? Suppose he understood Chinese! And if not, would the second voice be accepted as Grandfather's?

The Nipponese now made his wishes clearer by beckoning, and Thirty-nine poled the few feet back to shore. There the other stepped aboard, looked at the nets, peered for a long minute into the cabin at Old Head, then spoke again.

This last the grandson guessed concerned Lao To. In answer he pointed to the sleeping figure, tapped fingers against his own forehead—a sign understood in any language—and waited anxiously for the reaction. The pantomime proved satisfactory. With another careful glance about the deck, the sentry landed and gestured permission for them to proceed.

Slowly the youth pulled away. As on the day before, progress was blind, and holding the little craft to a safe course between shore and anchored vessels tested his skill to the limit. During all this time no sound had come from below deck, but now the Lieutenant cautioned in hushed tones, "Do not go too far from them!"

"I know," San-djiu replied, feeling like a fly in a spider web. With the pole having to cut each stroke through a thick wall of mist, it was impossible for the boatman to know where he was heading. If only the air would clear for a minute as it had yesterday to show the location of the warships! The mere thought of being so close to these massed enemy forces was in itself terrifying.

Meanwhile, the Lieutenant cramped beneath the floor was having his own problems. He dared not make himself more comfortable until sure of their position with regard to that of the enemy; also, no information could be procured while the weather remained as it was. Each passing hour would decrease the value of any detailed word to be carried into the city, then forwarded to the capital, Nanking.

Yesterday after leaving the cliffs, he had sent Ding at once to notify the authorities of Japanese arrival by sea and to obtain civilian garments for the two of them. In response to this alarm, those inside had so promptly barricaded the gates that the old soldier had apparently been forced to remain within the walls, for he had not returned. This particular development had not mattered greatly. Even the problem of civilian clothing was not too important. Whether a man was soldier or peaceful citizen meant little to these barbarians.

The officer possessed no false hopes about the value of his own present effort. Regardless of what might be learned today, he knew only too well that with the Fort gone, the city, a minor one, could not possibly combat a naval shelling or, for that matter, one by heavy land artillery. From his hideout in the fields the preceding afternoon, he had been able to see most of the equipment landed. It was chiefly small stuff and food supplies; what had to be discovered was whether larger ordnance would go ashore today. Obtaining the information, valuable or not as it might prove to the city, was of immediate importance to Nanking and he, as the Commander in Chief would have said bluntly, the only one to do it. His heart warmed at the thought of the Generalissimo, under whom he had trained at Whampoa

Military Academy. If anyone could lead China through this ordeal, Chiang Kai-shek was that man.

Thirty-nine's voice interrupted these memories. "I can no longer hear the sounds on their ships," he said.

Leaving cap and tunic below, the other crawled through the opening. "Since we started, I myself have heard nothing save waves against the boat."

"Naturally, down there."

"What did their sentry want?"

"Just to look at us. He must have been stupid or sleepy for he caused no trouble. At first, though, I nearly died of fright." After a second he added, "*Ai,* but their mouths do queer things when they speak."

"Like this, yes or no?" The officer stretched his own lips in imitation, and was rewarded by a grin from Young Li who now turned to drop anchor.

The present was the time for the youth and his grandfather to make their escape, the Lieutenant reminded himself. Once the air cleared, the little boat would be under constant surveillance. Indeed, the more he thought along this line, the more uncertain seemed the accomplishment of a landing up the coast. Someone aboard the warships had undoubtedly been told to watch all Chinese fishermen. With binoculars to help detect surprise moves and with motor launches for pursuit, the enemy held all the best dominoes in the game.

"Why did you anchor here, Li?" he asked suddenly.

"You wish to see what they do, Sir, not so?"

"In the fog escape is easier," countered the Lieutenant, waving the question aside.

"You mean, Sir, to leave before you find out what they have?" Puzzled, the youth frowned, then went on firmly, "If what you learn will harm them and help China, *muh iu fa tz!*"

"Li, you are a good citizen," returned the other approvingly. To himself he added, "When every man, woman, and child in this land feels as this boy does, our country need fear no enemy, however powerful."

Like all other officers in the Nationalist Army he had been prepared for an adversary far better equipped for modern warfare than were their own forces. China had one thing only—men. Accordingly, the Generalissimo recognizing that human beings, however courageous, have no chance against shells and bombs, had used every means possible to put off the evil day of combat until sufficient munitions could be acquired. This policy had earned the leader bitter criticism; earnest but less well-informed patriots had called him "pro-Japanese" and "traitor."

Yet in spite of all Chiang Kai-shek's efforts to prevent it, war had come, the young man told himself bleakly. How it would end depended on many things. Should their people become unified in a common cause, they might hold out against the invaders for a long time, although handicapped by having only primitive weapons. And if the friendly democracies, America, Great Britain, and France, would supply them with modern arms as Russia, their neighbor was already doing, then History might some day have a different tale to tell.

Thirty-nine broke in abruptly on this thinking. "*Hao puh hao* (good not good), Sir, you hide a little? I felt wind on my face and the mist is not so thick."

The faint breeze continued, gradually dissipating the moisture. In another half hour both ships and shore line could be clearly seen. The youth reached for the nets, but before casting, asked, "Will this place do?"

Cautiously the officer's head and shoulders came into view. "Yes," he answered slowly. "Hidden here behind the matting I can see them, yet not be seen."

For an hour or more they remained there—the Lieutenant studying ships and landing parties, San-djiu fishing. Two or three sampans were now in view; one seemed gradually to be nearing them. When only a few yards distant it anchored, but before that happened the officer had once more disappeared.

Pretending to work, the two fishermen aboard the other craft eyed Young Li. Recognizing them as old neighbors he called a greeting. Ching, the elder, answered, "I told Lu absolutely, it was you," he said. "We thought you were killed so he would not believe me. Where is the Old One?"

Thirty-nine pointed with his chin toward the cabin. "His head has a sickness." Talking with these men again warmed his heart, but even they must not know about the Lieutenant. In order to avoid further questioning, the youth asked them, "You, too, fish for those others, not so?"

"What else?" returned Lu. Furtively scanning their surroundings he warned, "Have care! Japanese are on some of the sampans." Then he continued in a low voice. "Yesterday six came to the village and ordered us to fish for them. Lao Wen—he too had remained there—dared to ask how his family could live, did he not feed them. Before the words were cold on his lips, one of the 'dwarfs' ran the knife on his gun into Wen's belly. He did not die fast enough. They set him against a wall and each of the five others did what the first had done." At the memory the speaker's face twitched painfully. "May Heaven pity us— they are the Devil King's own sons!" he finished hopelessly.

Little by little Ching was widening the distance between the two boats with his pole. "If they see us talk together, we shall die like Wen," he muttered.

As they moved off, San-djiu thought unhappily of Wen. That had been a good man, always ready to spend heart on a neighbor. Remembering that he himself had nearly asked the invaders the same fatal question, made him feel sick.

Once more the Lieutenant resumed his watch. From the first moments of clear weather a steady stream of supplies had gone shoreward. After a little while he announced, "I have learned enough. Let us go!"

Thirty-nine obeyed promptly. He could now see seven or eight sampans—all familiar, but the thought that Japanese might be aboard any one of them worried him. Proceeding northward, he managed to keep at a safe distance from the rest; they, on their part, apparently paid scant attention to his progress. When the last boat had been outdistanced, he called to the Lieutenant, "Is it better that I stop to fish a little, or go on?"

"Wait, let me look!"

Here they evidently had the sea to themselves. True, at this moment someone on the ship might be training glasses on them, but that risk must be accepted. Everything in war was a gamble, and just now Fortune seemed to be offering them the opportunity to escape. "Go on!" came the command.

San-djiu began to pole with every ounce of energy in his body. "About two *li* before we reach the village," he told the other, "the shore turns. Once I round that point, they can no longer see us from the ships."

In time this break in the coast line became visible, and with swift, sure strokes the youth negotiated the curve. Absorbed by the demands this made on seamanship, he was startled beyond description when the officer warned sharply, "Lie down! Quickly!"

Thirty-nine dropped to the deck. On the shore a short distance ahead a small boat was beached. Beyond it, with backs turned to the newcomers, were two Japanese holding a sheet of paper in the air before them. They had evidently been lost in discussion over a chart of some sort, but now, suddenly aware of intruders, they wheeled toward the water and pulled swiftly at holsters. In the same moment the Lieutenant's shot rang out; it was followed by another. The first man crumpled to the sands. The second stumbled, straightened, and returned fire. Again the Lieutenant pulled the trigger, and this time achieved his aim, for the Japanese dropped beside his comrade and lay still.

The whole encounter had occurred so swiftly that San-djiu was dazed with horror. He continued flat on the deck, his throat working convulsively. Finally realizing that the fighting was ended, he rose, went to Lao To and found him unharmed.

The officer now commanded brusquely, "Land!"

Grasping the oar, Thirty-nine exclaimed, "Sir, your shoulder bleeds!"

"A small affair," was the reply.

On the beach the Lieutenant busied himself with the bodies, salvaging weapons and papers, including the chart. These were stuffed carefully in his waistband before he searched their boat and appropriated two knapsacks and a high-powered field glass.

"Pick up some heavy stones, Li!" he called. Then, "Help weight their garments—so that they drown."

"But—but already they are dead, Sir," stammered the other.

"If their comrades find them shot, our own people living near by will suffer greatly. Hurry!"

Li obeyed, tormented by a mixture of fears and superstitions. All of his life he had been taught that it was wiser to have nothing to do with the dead. He wished earnestly to harm the Japanese, but to fight evil spirits that even this moment might be hovering over these bodies was something else again, and chilled his blood. As he worked he glanced once or twice at the Lieutenant—ai-ya, that one was afraid of nothing!

Within a short time the bodies had been placed on their own boat, rowed out to deeper water and heaved overboard. Later the boat was set adrift.

"Now let us hurry to that village," urged the officer.

San-djiu needed no further prodding. Never had he liked any place less than the one they were leaving. Before his

very eyes two men had been killed, and he himself had
handled their dead bodies and helped throw them to the
Sea Dragon. Who could say what ill-fortune might result?
This was an affair, indeed!

Meanwhile, the Lieutenant sat in the cabin beside Lao To
and examined the knapsacks. These contained concentrated
food, bottles of water, compasses, flash lights, and the First
Aid kits for which the searcher had been hoping. Calmly
he opened one of the last, and, after sterilizing, bandaged
the flesh wound in his shoulder. Next he pulled the papers
from his belt. These, however, were in Japanese characters and help would be needed in translating them. Returning them to safety he stretched out full length on the
floor.

Since noon the day before the officer had not slept. Both
body and mind ached with weariness. Furthermore, the
walk back from this village to the city would be a long
one unless a rickshaw could be picked up somewhere along
the way. So small a country community as the one just
ahead was unlikely to have any means of transportation save
passenger wheelbarrows and they were of no use to him.
There was a highway with a bus service somewhere in this
direction, but such vehicles were always much too overcrowded by regular patrons to pick up chance travelers. At
least he could fortify himself with the food and drink in the
knapsacks, and after his information had been delivered to
the proper authorities, he would sleep the night through.

Fatigue doubtless was causing the black depression in his
mind. But today as he had watched those heavy pieces being

put ashore, envy had overwhelmed him. Here at the out-set of this struggle the enemy was far better equipped than China's forces could hope to be even after several years. These knapsacks, for instance, were a small item, yet they held everything a foot-soldier needed besides weapons.

Well, in a day and a night with nothing but a revolver and bare hands he had accounted for three of the "dwarfs." Could that record continue—he would be satisfied. His lips twisted wryly. Had he not been sitting in the cabin watch-ing the shore, the affair would have ended differently. Of a certainty the wheel of Life sometimes seemed to spin with-out aim. Perhaps tomorrow—Kuan-yin be thanked! his tomorrows were still tied up in the scroll of the future, and no strength need be wasted worrying about them.

Young Li was already making the boat fast to a small, deserted landing. The Lieutenant rose to his feet and sug-gested, "Suppose you see if Japanese are in that village be-fore I appear in uniform."

Within a few minutes the youth returned with the infor-mation that this community as yet had not only had no con-tacts with the enemy, but was surprised by the thought of such a thing.

"Only fishermen and farmers live here," they had told Thirty-nine. "We have neither silver nor other treasure to tempt warlords."

"Our village was the same," he answered, "but we are homeless nevertheless. By sea my sick grandfather and I came to this place seeking safety."

"Bitter, bitter!" said the old shopkeeper who seemed to be the Village Elder. "Tonight rest here and tell more of this affair."

"With us is a Chinese soldier. He wishes to return at once to the city toward the South."

"In this place we have no high regard for soldiers," replied the shopkeeper, "but if he leaves at once, it is no matter."

San-djiu bowed, thanked them for the offer of hospitality, and hurried back to the boat.

The Lieutenant had already selected the articles he wished and now pushed the others toward Young Li. "Wrap those things in your *pu-gai*, then throw the knapsack away. Otherwise, the first Japanese you meet may kill you for having it. Add the food to your supplies. The flash light and other foreign objects may be exchanged for money when you need it most." He paused, then with a warm smile, added, "What needs to be said I will say here. Do not remain in that village, Li. Tomorrow or the next day our enemies may seize it. To win this war they must first take all of China's coast. Follow some road inland to the farms—there a strong youth can find work to do."

"But Lao To cannot travel!"

"Go slowly. It will not be too difficult—people are always good to the old. And one thing I believe: if you remain here, soon both of you may be killed." Retrieving cap and tunic from below deck, he concluded, "This is a war, Li, such as our country has never known. Try to remember that and put China first in all you do!"

Fifteen minutes later the Lieutenant was out of sight on the highway. San-djiu, settling Lao To on a bed within the hospitable shopkeeper's home, wondered with mixed emotions whether he would ever see the officer again. The memory of all that they had shared in the past days would remain with him a long, long time. Some of the other's actions had shocked the youth beyond words, but as the soldier had taken trouble to remind—this was to be a conflict such as China had never known in all history. From the instant those two Japanese had been sighted, the Lieutenant had recognized that he must kill or be killed. Well, one thing was certain —his people could no longer believe, as they had been taught for centuries, that "Good iron is not used to make nails or good men, soldiers."

On his second trip to the shore, he stood inactive for several minutes weighted down by indecision. To follow the officer's advice meant giving up his home perhaps forever. He, Li San-djiu-tz, was a fisherman born to the hazards of the ever-restless, ever-fascinating sea, and his heart knew no desire to go inland. Moreover, what of the boat? To leave it behind was almost like leaving part of his body. Who knew whether the Lieutenant was right or wrong? There was no fort near this village to tempt the enemy. Of course if the Japanese wished to capture the whole coast—that was a different affair. An old saying now beat on his mind: "To dig up a tree, begin with the root!" "Begin with the root," that was what he must do.

Lovingly, his fingers moved along the edge of the cabin roof as he stared for the last time at the dark, curling waves that stretched between him and an apricot-shaded sky. Doubt-less one of these villagers would pay something for the sampan, and tomorrow he would lead Old Head toward some safer haven in the farm lands. With resolution Thirty-nine caught up his possessions, then turning toward the village did not again look back.

Part II. THE REFUGEES

CHAPTER VI

"To Hear Tales of Trouble Does Not Equal the Experience"

LIKE thousands of other small rural communities throughout China, the Village of the Confucian Temple was
picturesque, kindly, and dirty. It differed from the settlement on the Point by being closer to fertile fields, and beneath the fifty or sixty roofs dwelt as many farmers as fishermen. While these villagers lacked a military garrison as
market and the city itself was at a distance, they derived certain benefits from the presence of the temple in their midst.

This, an unpretentious building, had no priests such as
were to be found in Buddhist and Taoist places of worship.
Only at the Winter Solstice did the simple rooms really warm

67

to life with men's sacrifices to Shang-ti, Ruler of Heaven, and to ancestral spirits. On such occasions people from a radius of several *li* poured into the little settlement. Since they were of all types, some of their observances were degraded forms of the original austere rites of Confucianism; but usually sedate, scholarly figures outnumbered the others and imparted some of their own dignity to all that occurred.

For several days business flourished in the two or three local shops, and the villagers, most of whom could neither read nor write, enjoyed the pleasant feeling of being in close touch with learning and culture. These elevating contacts provided the high point in their life and influenced conduct throughout the year. As a result, gambling and other vices were frowned upon; even the bickering of housewives common to closely crowded communities all over the world here was seldom heard.

Perhaps this habit of peaceful living had given the inhabitants a false sense of security, for they refused to find in Thirty-nine's account any hint of danger to themselves. Sitting in the Elder's home with the chief men of the little place about him, the youth was aware that his words were falling on deaf ears. He might just as well have been a wandering story-teller relating an ancient tale of the Three Kingdoms so little were these kindly folk concerned.

"That we have no fort near us is good fortune indeed!" remarked the hot-water seller complacently.

"Also the city is less close," a farmer agreed.

"*Ai*, and we be poor men—an evil that in wartime changes to good," explained the grain merchant.

"Soldiers and crows are alike—full of alarms."

Exhausted and discouraged, San-djiu made a final protest. "Respected Sirs, this village is three times as large and prosperous as was my native place. To the Japanese rich and poor are the same. The Lieutenant said that they must first take our whole coast, otherwise they can never conquer us."

The Elder made patient comment. "When your years are as many as mine, you will know that soldiers and crows are alike—full of alarms."

One by one the callers departed, pausing first to lean over Lao To stretched comfortably on the Elder's own bed and whisper, "Pity him, pity him—and at his age!"

Weary though he was, Thirty-nine lay awake for a long time. Who was right, the young officer or these elderly villagers? Gray hair was supposed to be a sign of wisdom. But Lao To's head was white with the frost of age and *he* had believed that the Point would be spared attack. More than once during those days in the caves, the Lieutenant had said, "Li, China must depend on boys like you. Our parents think only of the past; they believe that the Nipponese and local warlords are the same. If our country can be saved, the young must do it."

Well, that one had known what to expect certainly! San-djiu reminded himself. With bare hands he had killed a sentry before the sentry could kill him. Hidden in a dirty fishing boat the officer had voluntarily chosen for himself discomfort and risk such as soldiers of other days would have endured only under force. What was more, that afternoon he had been prepared for trouble in a spot where none had seemed likely and by instant, cold-blooded action had saved the three of them. None of this was according to custom, for China through the centuries had considered war and warriors uncivilized, and proportionately few of her soldiers had been noted for brains or courage. In contrast this young man seemed to possess both, and he, Li Thirty-nine, having earlier made the decision to follow the other's advice would not now change it. Where to go was the real problem. Wondering about this, the youth fell asleep.

Over morning rice he told the Elder of the intention to leave. At first the other seemed surprised, then with his usual kindliness personally arranged the sale of the boat. No one in the community could afford to buy such a thing at an acceptable price, but two fishermen who were brothers made the best offer. This was not one-tenth the value of a seaworthy sampan, but San-djiu was nevertheless glad to settle the deal. In his own mind there was the troubled feeling that any purchaser ran the risk of soon losing the craft to the Japanese; however, if after having heard his tale these people were still willing to buy, that was their affair, not his.

The news that the young refugee was leaving in spite of sage advice to the contrary surprised the villagers, and all who had not already gone to the fields or boats gathered to discuss the matter when the Elder and Thirty-nine returned from transacting the sale. Busy housewives caught up trays of vegetables or bits of mending on which they were working and sat in doorways in order not to miss what might be the only interesting moment in an otherwise dull day.

In squares marked off on the dusty road several small boys played a game using pebbles for counters. A six-year-old girl, freed for a moment from household tasks, kicked a shuttlecock deftly with her toe until she lost balance and sat down with a thud on the curbing. The small boys grinned, and the little maid, controlling swift tears, picked herself up and stalked off with childish dignity.

Several mangy dogs snapped at flies or searched vigorously for fleas, while a mother hen scratched dirt for food and clucked to her brood of chicks. At the sound of an invitation to eat, an old sow half rose from the ground, then with a short grunt of disappointment, sank back to her former position.

From a steaming vat the water seller ladled out a kettleful for a housewife, then tested the purchase coin by ringing it. Next leaning over the counter of his open shop he called to Thirty-nine, "Where do you and your Old One go?"

"Truly, I do not know," came the reply. "Perhaps someone in this Honorable Village can advise me. One thing I must do—find work in order to care for my grandfather."

From a doorstep an old woman cackled ironically, "Where is the farmer who will hire strangers to till his soil?"

"What you say, Old Mother, is true," commented the water seller. "Only in cities do men foolishly trust all who come and go."

"And how far is the nearest large town?" asked Thirty-nine.

"There is of course the city to the South; otherwise one must travel inland perhaps two hundred *li* or three."

Thirty-nine's hopes fell. "Lao To could not walk so far," he objected. To himself he wondered how with one pair of arms he could lead the old man and carry, even on a pole, *pu-gai*, charcoal stove, kettle, foodstuffs, and other articles. Yet no matter where they went, all of these things would be needed. In the country even the rich who could afford to stay at inns carried their own bedding and foodstuffs on journeys.

The screech of a creaking wheel suddenly interrupted the conversation. With spraddled legs and bent shoulders a barrowman pushed his awkward conveyance to the grain-merchant's shop and there set it down. After unloading several baskets of rice and millet, and receiving the fee, he squatted beside the step, untied a sweatband from about his head, and mopped hot face and shoulders.

While the villagers exchanged greetings with the new arrival, the food vender, who had been sorting long green cucumbers gave one to his two-year-old son. After this he suggested to San-djiu, "About thirty *li* from here my cousin dwells. Follow our path to the highway, next the first turn to the right. In time you will reach a small village. Pass it and go on to the second, which is larger. There ask for Chi Farmer, the father of six sons."

"Six sons!" exclaimed the old woman on the step. "Truly his fortune is great!"

"Also he has a good heart, though I his cousin should not boast of it," continued the first speaker. "When you say that I sent you, he will invite you and your Old One to remain for the night under his roof. Then, perhaps my cousin can advise you what to do."

Thirty-nine bowed. "Truly I am unworthy of such kindness!" he said gratefully. "There will we go."

For Grandfather to travel thirty *li* would require a number of days, the youth told himself, so they must start without further delay. Turning to the Elder to ask a question, he was interrupted by the wheelbarrow man's announcing, "A short distance beyond that village is my home. If you wish to ride to Chi Farmer's, I can carry you there."

Thirty-nine hesitated. Never had he traveled anywhere ashore except by his own feet. It was true that on his body at this moment was the silver from the boat sale, but that would justify no foolish extravagances. On the other hand, the sooner he reached some destination where a living might be earned the better, and to ride this first part of the journey would certainly benefit Lao To. "How much?" came the question.

The barrowman named a price, and at once all present entered the argument about fare. Finally, as was customary, the haggling ended in compromise. The youth now showed his appreciation of the food vender's suggestion by purchasing from that worthy two small packets of ginger root and nuts. These he presented to the Elder in acknowledgment of hospitality, then carefully expressing gratitude to the assembled community, prepared to depart.

To right and left of the protecting framework on the great wheel was a flat, slatted surface. On one of these the baggage was secured; on the other rode the two passengers. This made an unbalanced load, so the bearer shifted the supporting strap across his shoulders and tilted the wheel at an angle to adjust weight before pushing off.

With the help of the torn *pu-gai* to soften jars, the old man reclined as comfortably as was possible against the framework and his grandson's shoulder. San-djiu soon became accustomed to the rough movement of the iron tire on the uneven road, but the more severe jolts disturbed Old Head. Two or three times his eyes opened and seemed for a moment to lose their clouded expression, but he soon relapsed again into stupor.

On reaching the highway's smoother surface, the barrowman increased speed, and Thirty-nine began to enjoy the unfamiliar excitement of journeying. He had been too often to the city near the Point to be greatly surprised by the sight of motor vehicles, although these had not been numerous. For that community, which a century earlier had been important enough to warrant protection from a garrison and fort, had in modern times lost most of its trade to the great metropolis, Shanghai. At present, it was in reality not much larger than a thriving country town, with means of transportation still limited chiefly to rickshaws and load-bearers. Here on this modernized road, conveyances of every description passed to and fro, making progress difficult for pedestrians. A great lumbering bus whirred northward, honking violently for a clear way. San-djiu longed to ask where it was bound, but the barrowman was wasting no breath in talking; all his energy was needed to push the vehicle and avoid other traffic.

Eventually they turned right into a broad country lane. On either side fields were lush with crops. The deep black soil of the Yangtze Delta made a rich bed for rows of waving gold and green, and everywhere men were to be seen at work pedaling waterwheels or cultivating with sharp iron hoes. In one field a family harvested grain, their figures moving like shadows behind the screen of flying chaff.

With forced spurts of energy the barrowman climbed small camel-backed bridges over canals, then swiftly descended the sides sloping down to the road. Accustomed to a restless, powerful sea, Young Li found these quiet inland waterways strangely peaceful. Flat workboats or small fishing craft, on which trained cormorants did the work for men, floated by lazily. Watching these ugly birds dive into the water and bring up glittering spoils was a sight, indeed, for a fisherman used to toiling with nets.

"The collars about their throats keep them from swallowing the catch, not so?" he asked the barrowman.

"What else? For each big fish brought up, the owner feeds a small one to the bird."

"Would that Grandfather might see this affair!" Thirty-nine exclaimed, and with that the conversation ended. In the distance an occasional blue hill reached toward a paler sky, and on one of these a tall pagoda stood, stiff as a sentinel on duty guarding the great checkerboard of patterned farms.

By high noon the travelers arrived at the first village. Here they stopped and entered the inn. This was small and dingy but its cool shadows were a relief after the hot sunlight outside. The proprietor offered the customers a steaming towel with which to wipe their faces, and waited for an order. Thirty-nine, torn between thrift and Old Head's need of refreshment, listened to the barrowman's request for tea, then chose hot water, aware that Grandfather, though he ate and drank obediently, was still unable to know one thing from another. Their host raised an eyebrow over this frugality—it was his belief that anyone who could ride could certainly afford to eat well, but the thought did not find expression.

Later he asked the barrowman, "Did you meet those soldiers on the road?"

The other looked startled. "What soldiers?"

"Sometime before you arrived four or five tens of them passed."

"Did all wear uniform?"

"All wore uniforms, Kuan-yin be praised! No farmers had been seized; though when we saw them coming, our young men hid. It was wasted effort; the military did not stop—not even to demand free tea."

"For soldiers, *hsi chi deh hen*! (Strange, indeed!)" replied the customer, then after a thoughtful pause added, "This morning when I left, my son of seventeen years remained to till the field."

The innkeeper nodded understandingly. "All parents shake with the same fears when soldiers appear. Many people have said that these National Government fighters are different from the old ones—perhaps they are right."

Listening, Thirty-nine became uneasy. He knew far better than these two that Chiang Kai-shek's men were different, but every army had to add to its forces constantly and if this war continued as the Lieutenant expected, before long seventeen-year-old farm boys might not escape military duty so easily. He himself had sometimes been thought older than fifteen, and for Lao To's sake they must seek refuge off the beaten track, where soldiers were less likely to come.

Mid-afternoon found him and Old Head at their destination, and Chi Farmer proved to be all that his admiring cousin had suggested. Under the spreading roofs of this country house a short distance north of the village lived a large family and many helpers. To take in two more made little difference one way or another, and almost before Sandjiu could realize it, he and his grandfather had been given shelter in a shed at the rear.

The womenfolk made a great to-do over the old man, and the youth with his exciting story was the center of interest at evening rice with the men of the house. Chi and his stalwart sons listened attentively, but Thirty-nine soon recognized that these people also refused to see any danger to themselves in the present conflict. This village was not far from the north bank of the Yangtze and news of trouble on the coast came to them daily over the radio in the tea shop. But like country people elsewhere, they were comforted by the belief that so long as towns and cities offered opportunities for looting, no aggressor would waste strength on them.

The fourteen-year-old son alone seemed disturbed by his family's lack of concern over Thirty-nine's account. Hsiao Pan (Small Fat One), a name that natural plumpness had won for him, was the favorite with everybody about the farm. This was due not only to his being the youngest but also to a gay and mischievous manner. Now, even as his chopsticks worked rhythmically, pushing food from rice bowl to mouth, the boy's bright black eyes darted constantly from Young Li to the others. Finally he set down the emptied dish, wiped greasy, red lips on the back of his hand, and addressed Chi Farmer sagely, "Respected Parent, good or not good, we think of this matter a little? For almost two moons the Government air machine at the tea shop has been warning us of such trouble."

"Truly!" agreed an older brother impatiently, "that machine speaks of nothing else. The Japanese have seized the North, the Japanese attack Shanghai, the Japanese will conquer all China!" He snorted. "Are not our people five or seven times as many as the 'black dwarfs'? Talk, talk, talk! I, for one, no longer listen."

Hsiao Pan stuck into his mouth several grains of rice salvaged from the edge of his bowl, then replied with mock humility, "For one of your great wisdom to listen is needless, but for the rest of us—*muh iu fa tz!*" His hands gestured expressively.

Laughter rang out in response to this impudence, and the older one reached swiftly toward his tormentor. But Hsiao Pan, adept in eluding punishment, had already slipped from the bench and was safe on the way outside.

The father's eyes twinkled even as his tongue clicked in reproof. "This youth from the Coast will think we know no polite custom!" he told his family, then rising, stretched in a yawn and added, "Now I go sleep. War or peace, tomorrow that field to the south must be planted."

The next morning Chi Farmer offered Thirty-nine temporary work. The oldest son of his house was to be married in three months, and extra help would be needed in preparation for the wedding. "What better plan than to accept a youth already here?" he asked with a kindly smile, then added, "moreover, the women under my roof are agreed your Old One must not at present journey farther—is there more to be said?"

For three moons Li San-djiu-tz and his grandfather dwelt in this home. Never in fifteen years had the youth eaten such good and varied food. Lao To had spent money on meat only for Feast Days and that had been little enough. Here pork or fowl appeared frequently and on special occasions sweetened cakes or preserved ginger were an added treat. During the first fortnight Thirty-nine found himself constantly amazed by the presence of these luxuries. The only farmers he had known had been poor as fishermen. Chi was certainly not wealthy, for he and all his household worked unceasingly from dawn to dark; the farm, however, seemed to supply most of their needs in abundance. Fields were always green with rotating crops, and in season apricots, peaches, *pi-ba* (a small fruit tasting somewhat like a nectarine), and plums were plentiful. Truly, as the old woman in the village had said, Chi's fortune was good indeed.

Due to nursing and coddling by the women of the house, Lao To improved steadily. He slept less and speech slowly returned to him. As yet the old man seemed undisturbed by the changes in his life and he accepted San-djiu's simplified explanations without comment.

Meanwhile, the grandson worked diligently. Tilling the rich soil of the Yangtze Valley was very different from struggling with their own sandy patch on the Point; also this and every other task, however laborious, was lightened by the good humor that all under the roof seemed to share. The deep laughter of strong, contented men and women rang out at the most unexpected moments as they moved busily about the day's work. The old saying, "When a family lives in harmony all they do prospers," was certainly true in this instance.

Cultivating under the hot sun, Chi was fond of singing the farmer's song from the days of Yao and Shun, China's ancient kings, whose reign had been a Golden Age of peace and prosperity:

"I begin to work at sunrise
I do not rest until sunset
I drill my own well to get water
I till my own fields to get food
What then has the Emperor to do with me?"

Though the words meant little to him, Thirty-nine sometimes found himself chanting with the others this rhyme of independence to the swing of the hoe or the turns of the waterwheel. The names of Yao and Shun revered more than thirty centuries for goodness had been familiar to him all his life, but aside from fragmentary tales he knew nothing of national history. The Generalissimo's men at the Fort, and later the Lieutenant, had said that kings and emperors belonged to the past and that China was now a republic.

Once when he had asked the meaning of this word, someone had told him that it was a government like those of the

pink-skinned foreigners, called French, English, and American. In their countries which lay many thousands of *li*
beyond Nippon in the Eastern Sea, all men, it was said, were
equally important. Whenever he had seen these strangers in
the city, they had seemed very queer; why his own race
should copy any of their ways was beyond him. As for all
men being equally important—that was laugh talk, indeed.
For instance, was there no difference between him and the
Provincial Governor? *Ai-ya!*

Now such questions had become unimportant. One statement by the Lieutenant stood out above all others: "Facing invaders as powerful as the Japanese, our nation must
either unite or perish!" From this village Shanghai was less
than one hundred *li* distant, yet none of these people seemed
concerned about what was going on there, and he, an ignorant
newcomer, had no power to influence anyone except perhaps
Hsiao Pan.

No two youths could have been more unlike than San-
djiu and Hsiao Pan, yet they became immediate friends.
For the fishing-youth such companionship was a new experience. There had been a few boys of his own age on the
Point, but all worked as hard as he did. His own occasional
moments of leisure had been spent with the men at the Fort
or with Lao To, and he had never even imagined the sort of
carefree existence this youth lived. Chi Farmer permitted
no laziness in anyone about him. The youngest son did his
full share of work, but in every other way he was privileged
indeed. Although his brothers seldom lost an opportunity
of teasing Small Fat, they saved him from the brunt of

the most difficult tasks. Chi Mistress and the two unmarried daughters gave him dainties that the others never
glimpsed, and even the helpers about the place did everything that they could to make life easier for this half-grown
youth.

Whenever possible the two boys managed to labor side by
side; in free moments they slipped off together to hear the
radio in the village. News of government activities and the
progress of the war was mixed in with entertainment. Occasionally some stirring tale from China's long history fanned
listeners' patriotism to fresh flame. Hsiao Pan liked these
programs better than anything else. One night after hearing
how farmers in the Yuan Dynasty (1280-1368 A.D.) had
formed guerrilla bands and driven the Mongols out of China,
he was gravely silent on the way home.

"What affair is this that you save so much breath?" demanded San-djiu as they neared the farm.

"I have been thinking a little. Li, if our ancestors could
do that, so can we."

"Perhaps the Mongols did not have such powerful weapons
as the Japanese."

"True, but the Mongols already sat on the Dragon Throne
at Peking and ruled the whole country. So far the Japanese
fight only at the Coast and in the North."

His companion refused to acknowledge any hope in the
present situation. "You have never seen what their 'vulture
eggs' can do," he said dubiously.

As time passed, however, the fishing-youth began to realize why Chi Farmer and his neighbors were not more fearful

about the ominous news that reached them. Under the satisfactory living conditions of this fertile plain he himself in
spite of past evil experience felt horror gradually loosen
its grip on memory. Shelter, a full belly, and good companionship did much toward making men contented, he was
forced to admit.

Not until the end of their second moon in Chi's household
did shadows begin to deepen over this community. On a
number of occasions small groups of soldiers passed through
the village on their way, so it was rumored, to Shanghai.
As always in rural districts, the sight of uniformed men was
disturbing but when these caused no trouble, the farmers
promptly forgot them. This was particularly true of the Chi
Family, whose every effort was concentrated on the wedding.

Thirty-nine and Hsiao Pan alone worried when this military activity increased. Recently the radio had informed
them that affairs were going badly for China at Shanghai,
and they both wondered what a defeat there might mean.

Ten days before the marriage was to be consummated,
Young Li went on an errand to the village and there found
his worst fears realized. Huddled in the road about the
pitiful remnants of what had been cherished household possessions were thirty or forty strangers of all ages and varying conditions. Several had already stretched out in sleep
on bundles of bedding, and the others, a number of whom
wore stained rag bandages, sat desolate and silent where
they had first dropped to rest.

Three people knelt weeping beside an old man whose
breath came in ever-shorter gasps; and off to herself at the

roadside a young woman, her upper garment spotted with blood, hugged a dead baby to her breast and stared stony-eyed into space. Only in the bombing of his own village had Thirty-nine seen so much misery at one time, and his heart sank, guessing as he did the sort of tale these *t'ao-nan-tih* (fleeing-trouble-people) would have to relate.

After repeated questioning from the excited villagers, a middle-aged newcomer volunteered the information that all of them had dwelt not far from the south bank of the Yangtze; they had been forced to flee from the enemy, and in doing so many had been wounded and some killed.

"*Ai-ya!*" exclaimed the listeners, "for what reason? Were soldiers with you?"

"No. But soldiers or peaceful citizens, to the Japanese all are alike. The fault was ours—we waited too long," admitted one of the fleeing-trouble-people. Suddenly the story seemed to pour from his lips. "When Shanghai was attacked, many of our friends and neighbors sought haven in the foreign districts of that city where the 'dwarfs' did not dare to go. We, however, believed it wise to remain at home. Five years ago these men of the Eastern Sea waged war on Shanghai; nothing happened to us then, therefore why squeeze heart now? we asked ourselves. In time they would go away as they had before." He paused sadly. "This was not so. Then when Shanghai fell ——"

"Has Shanghai fallen?" exclaimed several villagers in the same breath.

It was the refugee's turn to be surprised. "Five days since. Does this place have no radio?"

"Yes, but for several days it has been useless. After Shanghai, what happened?"

"The enemy came inland on the way to Soochow. It was said that they were on the south bank only, so all in my house fled to the river, where we hoped to cross on a ferry. But there were many people and few boats. Also, enemy ships were on the Yangtze and their planes darkened the sky. Boatmen were afraid; like us, they hid in the sedge along the shore. Two days and two nights we waited, then one boatman, more daring than the others, offered to ferry some of us in the Hour of the Tiger before the sun rose. As we neared the northern bank, the sky lightened. One of their planes was above. Seeing us, it came closer and fired. When the machine flew away, five in our boat were dead—the others are here."

"*Ai*—this is a dreadful affair!" exclaimed a villager. "Those men from the Eastern Sea are devils, indeed!"

"Now where will you go?" asked another.

"Who can say? West, perhaps, to the nearest city to earn food," the refugee replied hopelessly. "For instance, when they arrive here, where will you yourselves go?"

"Arrive *here*—what talk is this?" demanded the villagers in consternation.

The other's lips twisted wryly. "Do not forget—we also thought they would not come near our homes. When even Government troops cannot stop them, can farmers do so?"

Listening, Thirty-nine felt sick at heart. Always it was the same—men refused to believe that what had harmed others might also harm them. He turned away and after completing his errand, followed the path slowly back to the farm.

There the others listened gravely to what Young Li had to relate. Today for the first time Chi Farmer seemed deeply worried.

"But there were no soldiers in that boat—how then could such a thing happen?" asked the eldest son.

His parent's brows knit together. "Truly, I do not like this tale! As soon as you are married," he promised, "we must find out what is really happening in our land. The present trouble seems more important than I thought."

For once Hsiao Pan had nothing to say, and while the family discussed the matter further, San-djiu slipped away by himself to think. At once Lao To must be moved somewhere else. If the Japanese had soldiers on the south bank and ships on the river, they would probably soon be here. But to leave now when Chi Farmer needed him most—*ai*, that was the difficulty! For three months he and his grandfather had received kindness beyond measure from this household. Chi's good heart had made the future wedding an excuse for sheltering two homeless refugees; there was no other reason. And now—Thirty-nine's head ached with the torment of this problem.

After a while he decided to risk staying on until the ceremony was over. There was a small stream that served as boundary line between the Chi Farm and several other places. Along the banks grew many rushes. These when thoroughly dried out would be used as winter fuel. As yet they had not been gathered and would still provide a good hiding place should such be needed. This very evening he would go and select one of the drier spots for Lao To's use in emergency.

Suddenly Hsiao Pan appeared. "At present, you plan to take your grandfather elsewhere, yes, not yes?"

"Not wrong!"

"When?"

"After the wedding."

The other kicked at the dirt and picked up a pebble between his toes. "Suppose the Japanese come here before that time?"

There was a moment of silence, then San-djiu counseled lightly, "Lay down your heart!" Even as he said it, the thought of leaving this household and, in particular, the boy beside him seemed too much to bear. As if in challenge to their unhappy thoughts, the golden afternoon appeared radiant with promise. Much remained to be done before sunset, and turning they strode swiftly over the dusty path to the farmhouse.

Like luggage too tightly packed, each hour now bulged with innumerable tasks connected with the coming event. Two days before the ceremony Thirty-nine's entire time was spent feeding straw and stubble to the great stove in the kitchen that the iron caldrons embedded in its clay surface might supply baths for everyone. To the fire tender this seemed a reckless waste of both fuel and water, and not for one instant did he dream of being included in the cleansing program. Accordingly when told that evening to smother the fire and use the rest of the water on himself, he was startled beyond words.

Heretofore his bathing had been limited to a basin and a rag, or to the plunges in the sea occasionally demanded of fishermen. At such times had anyone told him soaking in hot water was pleasant, he would have acknowledged tolerantly that doubtless there were many other enjoyable experiences in life—could one afford them. At present in the Chi kitchen, however, it was clear that the mistress meant him to bathe, for his murmured protest was immediately waved aside.

"Must our guests stick blossoms in their nostrils so they do not smell pigs and chickens when you are present?" she scolded. Then because this good-natured farm wife could seldom remain stern more than a breath's length, her lips twitched with humor as she continued, "Moreover, wash your neck well and when the barber comes here tomorrow morning you, too, remember to be present!"

Hsiao Pan was an amused spectator of the bath that followed. In the middle of it Thirty-nine inquired plaintively, "Truly, do you yourself like all this wetness?"

The other, who seemed always to have an unlimited supply of salted watermelon seeds concealed on his person, now cracked one between molars, spat out the tough casing and chewed the kernel with relish. "There are pleasures I prefer. But once in a while—can do! The women under a roof worry greatly about such matters. If washing my skin on special occasions pleases them—*muh iu fa tz?*" he finished philosophically and cracked another seed.

The next morning the barber appeared as scheduled. When the other men had been attended to, San-djiu's head was shaved, washed, and rubbed with an oil that smelled pleasantly of flowers. Tweezers pulled stray hairs from his brows, and round cotton puffs on thin sticks thoroughly explored his ears. While he endured these efforts in his behalf with an air of martyrdom, the results were nonetheless amazing. His skin, for instance, was much whiter than he had supposed it to be by nature, and he now felt assured that no guest would have to use nostril blossoms because of him.

Also, in order that even the helpers in the household be suitably arrayed for the festivities, Chi Farmer had presented the youth with a complete new outfit. This consisted of blue cotton trousers neatly fastened at the ankles, a short coat of the same material, white socks and black sateen shoes. To have all new garments was surprising enough, but to possess a pair of shoes was unbelievable; in fifteen years of living he had gone barefooted except when severe weather necessitated using straw sandals.

Cleanliness and decent clothes together gave Thirty-nine an unusual sense of well-being and self-respect. No longer did his appearance suggest a poverty-stricken fisherman. Instead, it seemed highly possible that Fortune might in time lead him into much more profitable paths than those of the past.

On the wedding morn a steady stream of friends and relatives began filling the farmhouse soon after dawn. The presence of so many visitors would have turned any ordinary day into one of bustle and excitement. As it was, these guests in holiday dress and mood merely served to provide colorful background for more important activities. In the forenoon the groom departed on the ceremonial call to the home of his betrothed. Several hours later his return was followed promptly by the arrival of the bride's dowry. This consisting of twenty-odd chests and baskets borne by chant-ing load-bearers was exceeded in interest only by the ap-pearance of the red wedding chair in which rode the young woman herself.

The general gaiety was contagious. Sharing in this, San-djiu felt no premonition of disaster as the day wore on into night. The feast was now at its height. Ordered to bring a fresh bowl of browned sweetened pork to a table, he hurried over the outside path toward the kitchen and mid-way ran into Hsiao Pan. "*Ai*! what are you doing here?" he exclaimed.

"Li, listen a little!" came the urgent reply.

Thirty-nine halted abruptly. Straining to separate the assorted sounds of merriment, he murmured questioningly, "More firecrackers?"

"Do you forget we used the last an hour ago? Those are guns—shooting near the village, not so?"

San-djiu felt as if caught without a jacket in a wintry blast. Without another word, the two ran over the path to a point from which the settlement could be clearly seen. As they reached there, more shots rang out, a roof flared into flame, and the accompanying screams of terror and agony left no further doubts of what was happening. The enemy had come.

As they raced back home, Hsiao Pan said between breaths, "*I* will tell my father. You go at once to your Old One."

The grandson needed only a minute or so in which to gather up the *pu-gai* and a few other articles, swing the bundle over his shoulder, then lead Lao To to the selected hiding place among the rushes. There with the old man comfortably rolled in bedding, he sat down beside him to watch. This was his particular responsibility, and with so many male relatives about, Chi Farmer did not need the services of an extra youth for anything he might decide to do. And what could countrymen do with hoes and rakes against guns and bayonets? From where he hid, shadowy figures could already be seen moving silently over narrow field paths. Some were probably guests making abrupt departures; the others, women of the family being taken, like Old Head, to some place safer than the house.

The night air in this eleventh moon was crisp and the sky, its dark pattern irregularly flecked with gold, seemed still and serene. A few feet away the little stream ran on its destined course to deeper waters. Only two enemies did it have—drought and burning skies, but until another summer came to stay these offered no threat of danger. Of all Nature, the rushes alone crackling and soughing with each stir of air seemed in sympathy with man's suffering at this hour. Shivering, Young Li remembered that the bombing of the Point had been on a night as bright and peaceful. He reached for his own comfort—carefully patched weeks earlier by Chi Farm Wife's skillful fingers—then decided to leave it tied about their few things. It seemed wiser for him to sit here chilled than to risk even the slightest delay should they have to hurry elsewhere.

Through most of the endless wait Old Head slept warmly and comfortably. Once or twice when cries from the victims pierced even his eardrums, he roused to question, "What was that? Why are we not in our beds?" Easily satisfied by his grandson's replies, he was soon asleep once more.

In time the reflection from the burning village reddened the sky as far as eye could see. Hours passed before this faded to a dull glow and the screams that had made the night a horror gradually hushed. A little later Thirty-nine rose stiffly and looked toward the distant house. In the somber, smoky light it was impossible to distinguish more than a faint outline of the building. That there had been trouble he was certain. What had really happened, though, beneath that roof or whether the enemy still remained, there was no way for him to find out except by returning. While torn by concern for the Chi Family, he recognized that his going back there too soon might undo all previous efforts to protect Lao To. Instead, stretching wearily he sank down again to wait for daylight.

Meanwhile the Nipponese foraging party having plundered both village and adjoining farms had found the Chi homestead an unexpectedly rich prize. From there they carried away not only livestock and quantities of food, but whatever could be found of money or ornament in all that friendly company. Later some of the stolen earrings and bracelets found their way to Japan. The women who received and wore these modest trinkets doubtless never learned how great had been their cost in Chinese blood. For the marauders completing their work on that particular farm left behind the dead bodies of the owner, four of his sons, and a number of their friends.

Time whose successive years had brought only prosperity to this family had capriciously refused to let a wedding interfere with other more sinister plans. Fortune for Chi Farmer and all under his roof had finally ceased to be good.

CHAPTER VII

Li San-djiu-tz Talks with a Buddhist Priest

BY HIGH noon of that same day San-djiu and Lao To found themselves in a rural hamlet of six or seven houses about five *li* from the Chi homestead. Their arrival was promptly announced by barking dogs. This noise drew to the newcomers the attention of the inhabitants, most of whom were gathered together in the narrow roadway.

"Your name and whence do you come?" these demanded suspiciously. When the first questions were answered, they added, "Are you alone? And what is your business?"

"Whether others follow, I do not know," Young Li told them. "My grandfather has been ill and his strength is small—he must eat and rest before traveling farther. If some kind-hearted housewife will share food and drink with us, I will try to repay her."

"Shame!" exclaimed a stout middle-aged woman, named Su, "that fear makes us forget courtesy to the aged. Last night," she told Thirty-nine, "we heard soldiers' guns in the distance; after that the sky reddened. Our hearts were troubled but we went to bed—was there not work to be done at dawn? Then in the Hour of the Rat (11:00 P.M. to 1:00 A.M.) a stranger came this way screaming that his home and family had been destroyed. Naturally no one ventured out to question him, and after a little time all was quiet again. This morning my husband's younger brother found a dead man in his bean patch. Whether it was that one we do not know—the trouble to us is the same!"

"Who else but him?" challenged a man.

"Well, we shall know when Husband and Brother-in-law return from the next town. They went there," she explained turning to the youth, "to tell the Ta Lao-yeh (Great Old Ear, title for local official)."

"Perhaps!" admitted the man. "Though I myself think these newcomers may know more than officials of the affair."

"Then tell us!" another asked expectantly. "For it is an evil matter to find a dead man in our fields."

The stout woman interrupted again, "Have pity! First he and his Old One shall eat. A filled belly oils speech."

When the meal was over and Lao To stretched comfortably on a bed, San-djiu told his tale briefly. On the preceding night, he informed them, the "black dwarfs of the

Eastern Sea" had attacked the settlement a few *li* away, burning homes and killing people. He and his grandfather had managed to escape.

"But why come this way?" they wanted to know. "Seldom do we see a stranger; now in a few hours there are three, first the dead man, then yourselves. Most travelers follow the road to the South."

"For that reason I used the field paths. Our enemies also may be on the highway," replied the youth.

"Just as I said last moon on return from market town," reminded a young man. "There they could talk of nothing but a war in Shanghai. Here at home no one would believe me." He spat out fibers from the stub of sugar cane he had been chewing and added with a grin, "For that matter I myself did not believe it."

"And do they really fight at Shanghai?" questioned others.

"Already the Japanese have captured that city," San-djiu informed them.

A chorus of surprised exclamations greeted this statement, "Too hard to believe! Too hard to believe!"

"True, nevertheless!" returned the young refugee. More he would not say, in spite of the food supposed to oil speech. As it was, his throat ached painfully over the account. To relate the oft-told story of personal misfortune, or to mention the name, Chi, and the sufferings of that family was beyond strength. At the moment reality existed for him only in the nightmare of memory; his presence with Lao To in this tiny community, and the troubled discussion in which the inhabitants were engaging might all be, so far as the youth's tormented thoughts were concerned, but a trick of the imagination.

At dawn that morning, after waking Old Head and telling him to wait in the field, Thirty-nine had returned to the farm. There he had found the previously happy homestead changed to a charnel house. Of all the men who had been under Chi Farmer's roof, the eldest son, Hsiao Pan, and two laborers alone remained. That these four were still alive was due simply to their having had the responsibility of taking the women to a hiding place. Many guests frantically hurrying toward home had also been killed on the road. From one of the laborers San-djiu had learned these few stark facts. After his mind had managed to accept them, he had asked hesitantly, "And Chi Mistress?"

"What do you think? Naturally, she is half crazed. As soon as the dead have been properly cared for, she will be taken with Young Mistress and the unmarried maids to relatives in the Northwest. The sons remain here to till the soil."

"If the 'dwarfs' return?"

"We shall watch while working; when they come they will not find us."

"Would that I might stay with you! There will be too much for so few hands. And I can cook a little as well."

"A good heart but a bad plan! One thing *you* must do: take your grandfather to a safer place. Later, though, I will remember to tell the Eldest-born what you have said."

Suddenly conscious of a repeated question from these country people about him, Thirty-nine pulled himself back from that earlier experience to the present moment. When he had answered to their satisfaction, his thoughts wandered again to Chi Farm.

After talking with the laborer, he had gone to the shed to gather up the rest of his belongings. Not having entered the house proper and seen the destruction there, the youth had been amazed to find his own poor things ruined. Why soldiers should waste strength to break a cheap charcoal firepot, for instance, puzzled him. Finally, as he turned to leave, Hsiao Pan had appeared unexpectedly in the doorway.

For a long moment San-djiu had stared at his friend. In one night the other had bridged the broad gap between youth and maturity. His swollen eyes were now burned dry, and when he spoke it was in a tone from which light-heartedness seemed to have passed forever. "So they did not wait, Li, to suit our wishes?"

Thirty-nine, whose own eyelids were stinging with sharp pity, had been unable to find speech, and Hsiao Pan had continued, "Waste no more time here; you know how slowly your grandfather walks."

"And you?"

"Naturally, I stay with my brother. Like us, many of our neighbors will remain on the land."

"Should there be more trouble . . ." the sentence hung unfinished in the air.

"We must become like those farmers who fought the Mongols."

After a few more words they had said farewell, and San-djiu had started with Old Head on the journey to this hamlet.

The young man who liked sugar cane now announced abruptly to all about him, "Dead man or not in the Su bean patch, *I* go back to my vegetables. Already half of this day has been wasted."

"It may be wiser not to work while that stranger's spirit hovers only three feet above our fields," ventured a woman.

"Perhaps! But one question I would ask: is it wise to let those late cabbages rot for lack of picking?" With this retort he caught up a basket and moved toward a field.

One by one the others present now slipped away on personal affairs. Reaching for a piece of mending, the stout farm wife inquired, "Tonight, Young Li, where will you sleep?"

"Su Mistress, how far is the next village?"

"Perhaps five *li* or seven. Distance is best measured by legs. For you that is nothing; for your grandfather each *li* may seem twenty. Good, not good, you rest here? When my husband returns, he will wish to talk with you of these outside affairs."

The urgency to put more space between Lao To and their enemies made the youth refuse even while expressing deep appreciation.

"Well, if you must go, *muh iu fa tz*! Now listen a little! Before that village is reached, you will see a Buddhist temple in fields to the right. The Abbot is a good man. I am eight-tenths sure he will let you stay the night in one of the courts." She paused, clicked the metal thimble ring against her teeth, then went on, "Should he refuse and there is no other choice but the village, I warn you that innkeeper is a robber.

"Six years since my good man and I, returning from a visit to my parents' home, were forced by a snowstorm to stay the night under that rascal's roof. For supper and later a bed shared with five families of rats, he charged two dimes big money. Of course we both emptied our mouths of words but there was nothing to do except pay." She snapped off a piece of thread. "Two dimes *little* money would have been bad enough!"

Lao To stirred from his nap, and the farm wife murmured ruefully, "*Ai*—I have waked him! Sometimes my speech flows like 'China's Sorrow' (the Yellow River) in flood."

Protesting courteously that all her words were good, Thirty-nine rose and added, "Mistress, now we must go. How much do we owe for such great kindness?"

"Do not mention again so small a matter!"

"But I have a few coins to pay for food."

Her brows lifted in consternation. "Be more careful about telling the world you have a few coins, or soon there will be none!"

San-djiu, acknowledging this advice, continued, "We are most unworthy. May Heaven remember your good deeds!"

"It is nothing—nothing!" Then in the next breath she said shrewdly, "It would do no harm, however, if you mentioned my name to the priests at that temple, not so? Before this matter of the dead man is settled, we may have to call on them."

Promising to do this and again expressing gratitude for hospitality, San-djiu led his grandfather away. Lao To seemed refreshed by food and rest. When they made their first halt, he asked much to the youth's surprise, "Now tell me of our affairs!"

After the account was finished the old man sat silent. "At present where do we go?" was his next question.

The grandson told him of the plan for the night.

"We have how much money?"

Thirty-nine looked carefully about him. Several fields away men were scooping liquid fertilizer on the soil, and on a path close by a small boy riding a water buffalo switched rhythmically at the beast's flanks with a willow spray. Reassured, the youth drew the moneybag from within his belt. Passing it over, he said, "We have also those Japanese articles the Lieutenant gave me; when we need silver, they may be exchanged for it."

After counting carefully, Old Head seemed again lost in thought. What he would have done had his mind been clear through all the happenings, it was hard to know. However, this youth beside him had been bearing a man's burdens and perhaps his plan of coming inland might in the end prove to be the wisest possible. Glancing at Thirty-nine, the grandfather managed a gentle smile. "Truly, you have been faithful," he commended. "Now let us go on to this temple! After sleep we can talk again of these matters."

Dusk was deepening by the time they arrived at their destination. As the farm wife had predicted, permission for them to spend the night was readily granted. A kitchen novice brought bowls of tea and thick vegetable broth, then showed them where to rest.

Within a short time the services commenced.

Within a short time the regular eventide services commenced. From before the Buddha's shrine, the rich tones of a beaten gong called priests and acolytes to respective duties. The sound of chanting voices echoed through the courts and smoke from burning incense weighted the air. Outside, the fields lay hushed, and the temple's tiled arching roof and stout walls seemed to offer security to all who dwelt within.

Lao To, as usual, fell easily asleep, but his grandson tossed from side to side. Even the marked improvement in Old Head failed to lighten his unhappy mood. Like some farmer pedaling a water wheel, his thoughts retrod over and over each step of the day's experiences and completed the painful circle with the memory of his friend. That no one ever again was likely to use the affectionate nickname, "Small Fat," of the purposeful, embittered youth from whom he had parted in the morning, seemed important beyond all proportion. "Some day," he promised himself hotheartedly, "they shall pay for that."

But now his problem was where to go next. "Inland!" the Lieutenant had advised, and this they had done. At their slow progress, though, could the two of them hope to outdistance the enemy? Sixteen days had passed since the fall of Shanghai if what those refugees had told was true. Soochow had been mentioned as the enemy's next objective. That city was supposed to be very beautiful. There was even an old saying, "Above is Heaven; below is Soochow and Hangchow." His geography, however, was a vague assortment of names and directions, and all he knew of that city's location was that it lay south of the Son of the Sea (Yangtze River). At present he and his grandfather were north of the same river and nearly forty *li* from the Coast. Where to go from here or what route to use remained a mystery.

Physical exhaustion finally did its work. When San-djiu's eyes opened again, he was astonished to see daylight. At departure, after contributing a small coin as thank offering, he remembered the promise to the farm wife. For someone in his humble position to approach these priests required daring. He glanced about the hall. Most of the gray-robed, shaven-headed figures seemed to stand in groups of twos and threes, but over to the left, staring into space and fingering his beads, one was alone.

San-djiu walked hesitantly up to him.

For a moment or two the priest's hands continued running over the long chain of beads, then he asked quietly, "What do you wish?"

"To thank all in this temple, Sir Priest, for kindness to my grandfather and me. The wife of Su Farmer, in that hamlet five *li* to the East, told me to come here. She is a woman who does many good deeds."

"Thus do souls earn merit," rejoined the priest automatically and added, "you dwell in that place?"

"No, Sir Priest."

"You are pilgrims?"

"Refugees."

"I have not heard of flood or famine."

"We flee from men of the Eastern Ocean."

The expression in the questioner's eyes changed peculiarly for a second, then he went on, "In country temples one learns little of the outside world. Tell me of this latest trouble."

"They fight on the Coast. There our home was bombed, so we came inland. Last night the barbarians destroyed that other settlement. Therefore are we here."

The priest shook his head. "Too hard to believe that men could be so evil," he said and ended the conversation by resuming his prayers.

Afterwards on the road, Thirty-nine found himself recalling this experience in every detail. Something about it disturbed him vaguely, but whether connected with the questions or with the priest himself, he was not certain. Why so small an affair should assume such importance seemed beyond explanation, and eventually he pushed it into the background of his mind.

That afternoon Lao To's second discussion of their problems took place. When it was over the grandson felt more cheerful. With Old Head again sharing responsibility, future difficulties appeared much less formidable.

Through several weeks the two refugees plodded along secluded country paths. In the farming section they heard few references to war. As yet only the larger communities in touch with the outside world by radio seemed affected. In such places patriotic mass meetings were being held and youths conscripted for military service. But even in these settlements what the Lieutenant had predicted about kindness to the aged had proven true. The sight of Lao To's worn figure and white hair opened doors that would otherwise have remained barred to a lone, able-bodied youth.

Yet, in spite of care and thoughtfulness, the journeying was beginning to tell on the elder. His mind was still clear, but physically he grew weaker all the time. To save the other's strength, San-djiu spent precious silver on wheelbarrows or rickshaws whenever these were available. Then three days of exposure to drizzling rain gave the old man a bad chest cold, and finally one morning he was unable to rise from the bed in the inn where they had spent the previous night. As his grandfather's fever increased and breathing became more labored, Thirty-nine grew frightened. The youth had never had any dealings with doctors, but now he asked the innkeeper, "Is there a healer in this place?"

"Not now. He died two years ago and having neither son nor nephew, he had taught no one his work. In this village, when the old wives' remedies do not help, the patients die. *Muh iu fa tz!*"

"*Puh mang! Puh mang.* (Not too fast!)" broke in a customer, who was sipping tea at a table. "You forget the foreign doctor. Since he first visited us, many have recovered from their illnesses."

"Perhaps!" replied the innkeeper. "Though I myself think they would have improved anyway."

"Each man to his own thoughts!" granted the tea drinker tolerantly. "My cousin, however, who has the seven daughters and only one son thinks the foreigner works magic. When the boy became sick, priests were called in and, later, a doctor from the city. These efforts were useless. By the

time the other—he is an American—came on his next visit
to this place, the sick child's spirit was ready to ascend the
Dragon (die). Desperate, my cousin sought out the foreigner. Within a moon his son was again at school. Truly,
you must remember this affair!"

"Yes, I remember," came grudgingly.

From the entrance, a load-bearer interrupted, "Look at
my right arm! For two moons I could not carry. My family was starving. Someone told me to go to the American.
He gave me pills to eat. Can you believe it? Pills for a
stiff arm, and not one hot needle stuck in it! I told myself,
'For once the woman in your house is right. She said this
foreigner was a fool.' But to save face with my wife I went
home and ate his medicine." He smiled broadly. "We were
both wrong, for at once the arm began to mend."

"When does this outsider come again?" San-djiu asked
suddenly.

All present hazarded guesses but no one was certain. The
carrier's brows knitted in thought, then he said, "I believe
the healer arrives here tomorrow. If so, your fortune is
great."

That day and night of waiting seemed endless to the
worried grandson. By morning Lao To was definitely worse
and, unless help came from somewhere, it seemed highly
probable that the old man would die. Even the innkeeper,
who had so little faith in doctors, was now extremely anxious
for the foreign one to arrive. The proprietor was a good-
hearted man and he hesitated to tell these two poor customers
to go elsewhere, particularly since one was old and sick. On

the other hand, should the elder die here, business in this inn would be ruined for many months to come.

Just before noon, as the load-bearer had expected, the American Doctor Morland and a Chinese male nurse drove into the village. They stopped before a small boarded shop front and opening it, went inside. This building rented for clinical purposes by the hospital in the nearest city bore little resemblance to such places in Europe and America. The former shop was furnished with seats only; the living room at the rear had in addition a crude table for examinations. Medical equipment and drugs were much too scarce and valuable in the hospital itself to store any in a small rural center that was visited only twice a month. Walls, however, were bright with posters, and the colorful drawings never failed to be of interest even when patients were unable to read the characters written below. Many of the pictures proclaimed vividly the evils caused by mosquitoes and rats. Others were concerned with the National Government's New Life Program of Spiritual and Physical Hygiene.

Surprisingly enough, although the village had seemed unconcerned about the doctor's coming, within fifteen minutes after his arrival, the receiving room was filled with ailing men, women, and children. For a minimum fee these were examined, treated, and supplied with medicine.

Thirty-nine was sixth in turn. Sitting on the edge of a stool shared with an old woman he found much to think about. That yesterday he should have decided to ask this foreigner to look at Lao To still troubled him. No one in his family had ever had personal dealings with the pink-skinned outsiders, and to do so now seemed a questionable step. Only the firm belief that Old Head would otherwise soon die had forced the youth to take it.

He watched the two men move swiftly about their work. One thing was good: the physician did not look so queer as those others he had seen in the city near the Point. True, the man was very tall and, like the rest of his race, had a rather large nose, but his skin, hair, and eyes were almost as dark as those of a Chinese.

What was even more remarkable was his speech. San-djiu had supposed that the male nurse would do all the talking. This was not the case. Snatches of the doctor's conversations with patients drifted to his ears and puzzled him. Turning to his neighbor on the stool, the youth asked, "Lao Po-po (Old Grandmother), I do not know the foreign tongue, yet some of that healer's words are familiar. What language does he speak?"

The old woman stared at him between narrowed eye slits. "You are even more stupid than most of the young," she said frankly. "Do you not recognize Chinese when you hear it?"

Her blunt statement was no comfort to Thirty-nine who was steadily becoming more uneasy as his turn approached. When the Chinese nurse beckoned to him, then asked, "What is the matter with you?" the youth could only stammer, "Nothing, Sir, nothing!"

"Why come here?"

"My grandfather is very ill."

"Where is he?"

"In bed at the inn."

The nurse turned and called out to his superior. "Doctor, this boy says his Old One is ill at the inn."

The physician now came over to them for further information. Under his kindly questioning San-djiu's uneasiness lessened. A moment later he was on his way to the inn with the doctor's promise to visit Lao To when the work at the dispensary was finished.

Later after examining the old man, the physician said, "Your grandfather has a bad disease. Here I can do nothing for him. Moving him to the hospital may also cause death, but safely arrived in that building, he will have a small chance to live. This is your affair—what do you wish?"

Thirty-nine was aghast. He had expected this doctor to give Lao To medicine and thus cure him. The thought of going to a foreign hospital was terrifying. Moreover, such a thing would certainly cost more money than they could afford. His brain was whirling with doubts. The foreigner believed Old Head would die here. He might even die on the road, but in the hospital—*ai*, Kuan-yin have pity! What must they do?

At last he managed to ask aloud, "At the *Ih-yuen* (Healing Hall) how much will it cost?"

"Lay down your heart!" replied the foreigner. "If your money is not enough, perhaps you can think up a way to earn a little. Now, we must delay no longer."

Within a few minutes Lao To had been wrapped in the comforts and placed on the back seat of the car. His grandson sat on the floor beside him, torn between worry and the fearful excitement of riding in a foreign devil-machine. Crushed in his hand were two sesame seed cakes. The inn-keeper had been so relieved to see his sick guest leave that he had sped the three others on their way with a serving of tea and sweetmeats. Thirty-nine, suddenly aware of the cakes still clenched in his hand, began nibbling at them.

After a while the doctor called back from the driver's seat, "Now, Li, tell me about yourselves. A few things I must know."

By the time all his questions were satisfactorily answered they had reached the city and a little later arrived at the hospital entrance.

CHAPTER VIII

"In the Four Seas All Men Are Brothers"—Confucius

DURING the months that followed, San-djiu might almost have been on another planet so different was the existence of which he now became a part. At first, while Life and Death fought a grim battle over Lao To, he was concerned only with that struggle. After the pneumonia crisis was passed, and Doctor Morland told him that Old Head had a chance to live, the grandson began to interest himself in the surroundings.

The morning after their arrival at the Mission Hospital, Hu Ih-hseng, the young Chinese physician on the staff, turned the worried, aimless youth over to the gardener. At first this old workman, who loved each plant as if it were a child, did little but scold the new recruit. Farming and floral culture are two very different things, Thirty-nine found out to his dismay. Fortunately the season for outdoor blooms had passed, but chrysanthemums still flaunted their magnificence in long rows of ornamental jars in entrance hall and corridors. Learning to care for these and for rare potted shrubs, the former fisherman felt as clumsy as a water buffalo; however, as time went on his work improved.

The hospital, a square, foreignized building of gray stone with curving Chinese roof, was almost surrounded by lawn and flower borders. This still-green expanse was very pleasant to look at San-djiu admitted to himself, but he was able to approve of only one thing—the space at the rear that was devoted in season to vegetables. Each inch of earth High Heaven gave man to use, the poor of his land believed, was meant for producing food. To do anything else with it was to ask for misfortune. Only the rich and these foreigners had the daring to waste soil on other purposes.

Indeed, this was but one of many strange foreign ideas, and in those early weeks of association the young fisherman went about in a state of bewilderment wondering what next to expect. Before the bombing of the Point, when he had dreamed of seeking a more exciting fortune, it had been, naturally, among his own kind. That adventure might lurk in contacts with friendly aliens would never have occurred to him. Yet in the Healing Hall at Y——, sharing in a life so unlike that of the fishing village, Thirty-nine discovered gradually that not all men from beyond the sea were barbarians. Moreover, some of them, at least, possessed qualities similar to the best found in Chinese.

The hospital was of moderate size with admissions limited to men. Doctor Morland, Meng Ih-hseng as he was called in Chinese, was the only foreign physician and headed the staff. Hu Ih-hseng was his assistant. Miss Benton (Beh Hsiao-je), another American, served as Superintendent of Nursing; and Mrs. Morland (Meng Si-mu) acted as anaesthetist, secretary, and bookkeeper for the institution. Added to these were the Chinese male nurses, orderlies, and servants. While Y—— was a small city, its population, together with that of the surrounding countryside, kept the hospital staff busy beyond their strength—a common condition everywhere in China where medical workers were few in number.

In the beginning Thirty-nine studied his new acquaintances with a wary eye. He was suspicious even of Hu Doctor and the other Chinese on the force because of their intimacy with the three foreigners. They talked, laughed, and worked together not only as friends but also as if all belonged to one nation. For a Chinese country youth, this situation was difficult to understand.

As time wore on, however, their continued kindness to Lao To and the other sufferers in the Healing Hall changed his attitude completely. Of almost equal influence with him was the genuine concern of the three Americans over the war. He had, as yet, seen none of his own people display such deep anxiety at each announcement of Japanese gains. Why this was so the youth could not understand. Had someone told him that many outsiders felt as loyal to China as to their native lands, he would have thought the statement ridiculous. Personal experience alone would help him to realize that this was true.

The enemy, he learned soon after arrival at Y——, had succeeded in capturing Soochow and a number of smaller towns. Nothing now stood between the Japanese and their assault on Nanking save the exhausted, ill-equipped, and hopelessly outnumbered ranks of the retreating Chinese Army. On the southern bank, it was said, an endless stream of homeless, desperate people jammed all roads leading westward from the Coast. Thinking of these and recalling the pitiable refugees at the village near Chi Farm, he felt duly grateful for this haven into which he and Lao To had drifted.

For the first time since the destruction of the Fort, the youth had reached a community where the national conflict was the topic of supreme importance. This was true of city as well as hospital. Y——, a reasonable distance inland from the north shore, presented no particular temptation at the moment to an enemy occupied in seizing much richer prizes. But with word of Shanghai's defeat and the muffled sound of distant explosions constantly in their ears, the citizens refused to be complacent about location. Men of all ages were recruited and drilled for military service. Various civic groups made appeals for War Chest funds. Students from the schools held patriotic mass meetings and taught their audiences the newly composed songs on National Salvation.

Later on, Boy Scouts went from door to door with two official requests. The first asked that everything possible be salvaged in homes and contributed to government use.

As a race the Chinese consider waste of any sort unpardonable. Accordingly, this plea brought to the average householder a clearer realization of the seriousness of the conflict than did graphic accounts of active fighting.

The second request stirred up as much excitement as an exploding bomb. Wherever the enemy appeared in conquest, the Government hoped that citizens before fleeing elsewhere would destroy everything useful to the invaders. This included objects too large to be carried on the road, food and water supplies, and buildings of all descriptions. A special message to farmers asked for crops in their fields to be burned rather than left to the enemy. Retreating Chinese soldiers could be counted upon to help civilians in this "scorched earth" policy.

The people were horrified by such suggestions. From time immemorial whenever wars and natural disasters occurred, Chinese had been accustomed to leave their homes and come back as soon as conditions improved. If houses and furnishings were destroyed, what then would there be on return? they wanted to know. As for asking farmers to burn crops—that was unthinkable. For days little else was discussed. The National Government troops had better do something to check the Japanese instead of using strength to destroy good Chinese property, argued the civilians. *Ai*— what an affair! Only when an official explained the bitter, inescapable facts dictating this program of devastation, did public feeling begin to change.

Hearing these indignant comments not only among hospital servants and visitors but wherever he was sent on errands in the city, Thirty-nine wondered. Remembering what bombs had done to the Point and also the "dwarfs' " methods with his few possessions at Chi Farm, there seemed to him little need for citizens to waste effort.

Of course, if the Nipponese stayed on where they had conquered, that was something else again. In such cases doubtless everything would be seized for their use. Furthermore, once in possession, they would certainly not permit original owners to return and claim anything for themselves. It seemed quite likely, he thought sagely, that the Government knew what it was doing, though that business of farmers— *ai-ya*! Lao To firing a crop after laboring with it for months was too much for the grandson's imagination to picture. And when it came to growing plants, countrymen everywhere were just alike.

That before long farmers all over invaded areas would grimly and unfalteringly blacken each inch of their fields without waiting for help from soldiers was something that no Chinese would ever have expected to see performed. China was used to suffering. Her people through the centuries had endured the torments of war, conquest, plague, flood, and famine. Peace-loving by nature, they had accepted these evils and rebuilt patiently from ruins. At the hands of the Japanese, though, civilians and soldiers alike were experiencing a brutality unequaled in the several thousand years of national history. The conquerors counted on this course of action to terrify their victims into submission. Instead, it was swiftly to unite the entire Chinese people into a solid wall of resistance.

In Doctor Morland's office a radio, tuned low that patients might not be disturbed, kept the institution informed about what was happening in the war zone. Additional news came by way of the post. Some days when the uniformed carrier delivered the mail into the hospital gateman's hands, San-djiu thought the pile of letters and papers enough to satisfy the entire city. Certainly it was wonderful for men to be able to write, but that they should waste so much time doing it was amazing. In all his life he could not remember ten letters having been delivered on the Point.

The abundant mail soon gave the youth an idea: he would send a letter to his friend. Hsiao Pan recognized several tens of characters, and the older brother could help him read the others. Tomorrow on the street he would hire the services of a public letter writer, if the cost were not too great.

The following day one was located in an angle of wall at the intersection of two busy streets. Although timid about dealings with educated men, Thirty-nine had no intention of throwing money away needlessly, and a lengthy argument ensued over price. The bargaining was settled only when the customer recognized that no further reduction in fee would be made.

Meanwhile there had collected about the small table with its neatly arranged equipment a highly interested audience. Listening to the personal revelations in a sender's message and watching the scribe put them down on paper always provided fascinating entertainment for idlers. Two load-bearers with goods delivered and slack ropes hanging from their shoulder-poles arrived first. A tailor's apprentice, holding carefully to a folded muslin square in which was wrapped some customer's new garment came next, and was followed by several laughing schoolboys. An old grandfather sucking at a water pipe and a young man of fashion in mulberry satin who carried a pet songbird on one wrist completed the group.

San-djiu's face was red with embarrassment. He felt as if the whole city of Y—— were trying to find out how stupid he was. For the letter writer, accustomed to spectators, these others might not even have existed as he set calmly about preparations for work.

There was nothing hurried about the performance. He placed directly before him a narrow sheet of rice paper, with red lines running from top to bottom. Then moistening a brush pen on the square, flat slab of ink, he turned an attentive ear to his patron. As Thirty-nine, knowing neither what to say nor how to say it, stumbled over sentences, the other changed the wording to conform with what was proper and courteous, then wrote. Each character was formed slowly and with flourishes, much as if a picture were being painted— an artistic manner always appreciated by onlookers.

Suddenly one of the schoolboys, whose impudence left the youthful patron openmouthed, corrected the writer on the order of strokes in a complex character. The victim of this criticism paid no attention until the young man in the mulberry satin added, "It is true. That long stroke on the left should be made before the short one."

The work came to an abrupt halt. Laying down his brush and smiling much too pleasantly, the professional replied, "Gentlemen, a thousand pardons! To be honored by two great scholars—one not yet weaned—is more than I deserve."

At this sally the load-bearers laughed aloud and the schoolboys excepting the one "not yet weaned" joined in. The young man of fashion merely shrugged his shoulders, yawned affectedly and patting the bird, sauntered down the street. As he did so the grandfather with the water pipe turned to the first critic sternly. "Do your parents know no rules of propriety, that you correct elders in public?"

With family pride under attack the boy blushed but made no reply. A moment later he and his companions, pushing each other about like animal cubs, wandered on their way. After another pull at the water pipe, the Old One finished, "It is these new schools that spoil them. In my youth a boy would have tasted the bamboo (been whipped) for such rudeness."

Later, on the way back to the hospital, San-djiu chuckled to himself, recalling this affair. The argument had helped him forget embarrassment, with the result that Hsiao Pan would receive a longer letter than had seemed possible at the beginning.

Doctor Morland, with the customary black bag in his hand, met the youth on the graveled drive in the compound. Thirty-nine sometimes wondered when the physicians ate and slept; they seemed chained to a continuous round of duties. Yet the American was never too hurried to pause for a word of conversation. Now he said, "Li, your grandfather is better today. Soon we shall hope to have him well."

After expressing gratitude, San-djiu walked on with mixed
feelings. To his own surprise he admitted a growing attachment to this place and its people. Old Head's recovery was
the grandson's first hope, but at the same time, it meant the
renewed search for a permanent dwelling place.

That other circumstances were working to postpone such
a move he had no way of knowing. One morning Hu Ih-hseng
halted him in the corridor and after careful scrutiny said
thoughtfully, "Li, today you can try doing orderly duty in
the wards."

"Do what, Sir?" Thirty-nine replied in astonishment.

"Sung Orderly has not come, and the other man, Wei,
has too much work for one person." With a touch of humor
the Chinese physician continued, "First, though, we shall
have to labor a little with *you*. Bathe your body thoroughly!
Then ask the nurse on that floor for an orderly's white suit.
Afterwards he will tell you what to do."

The doctor started away, only to call back over his
shoulder, "Clean hair and fingernails are most important
always!"

In spite of being dubious about this sudden promotion,
Thirty-nine did as ordered without question. As long as he
was under obligation to the hospital, it would not enter his
head to raise objections about anything. And one thing was
certain—for a fisherman to become a hospital attendant
overnight must make even the gods laugh.

Bathing, he reflected in the tub, was a favorite habit of
the outsiders. Chi Farm Wife, for instance, had demanded
only occasional cleansings; these foreigners, according to

the servants, spent a good part of their lives soaking in warm water. In this, he told himself with a grin, they were like *shui-niu* (water buffaloes), which were happiest when only their nostrils showed above the surface of a pool. The amusing thought came to him that perhaps this constant washing was what made Americans whiter than Chinese. *Ai*—suppose they expected orderlies also to bathe once a day! It was comforting to recall that Hu Ih-hseng's skin, even though it smelled peculiarly of foreign soap, had not paled, and he took as many baths as the others.

Garbed in white, Li appeared a half hour later before the nurse and asked for orders. In the first ten minutes it became increasingly clear that this new position was a long step up in the world. Patients who had never even glanced his way when he helped servants move furniture now smiled in welcome and addressed him with respect. He was inexpert and clumsy, but the tasks were not too difficult and given time he would learn to do them well.

The next morning Hu Ih-hseng again called him aside to ask bluntly, "Yesterday, how many things did you break?"

"*Ai*, Honorable Doctor, so you knew?" Li asked in consternation.

The other's lips twitched. "Sometimes I have fortune-telling talent."

Sheepishly Thirty-nine confessed, "That fat merchant's tray of food fell."

"And he told you politely, 'Not important! Not important!' "

"Truly no! When insulting words gave out, he used them all over again. But what he said seemed guest talk when nurse and cook began. *Ai*—that cook!"

The physician laughed, then said surprisingly, "Work there again today."

"But, Honorable Doctor," the youth started to protest.

"Lay down your heart! You will learn. Just remember that dishes are not boats or nets." More seriously he finished, "Sung Orderly has gone to serve at the battle front. He will not soon return."

Working in the ward, San-djiu was free to see Lao To whenever opportunity offered. The elder, still too weak to talk very much, looked long at this clean, white-clothed grandson. In those peaceful days on the Point, Old Head had dreamed that the youth might some day achieve great things, and now the expectations seemed about to become facts. Within a few moons the other had made a most unusual advance. What was more—by personal effort the boy was paying in part at least for the benefits they were both receiving.

With mischief in his voice, Thirty-nine confided, "The patients think me important."

Lao To's eyes twinkled. " 'Beware of pride,' " he quoted slowly, " 'even the tiger has his naps.' "

Left to himself, the old man's thoughts shifted to the foreigners, who his generation had been taught were all barbarians. Perhaps this teaching had been only seven-tenths right. True, at present, the people of one country in the Eastern Ocean were killing Chinese everywhere, but

those from another worked equally hard to save men of
the Middle Kingdom (old name for China)—his own case
was an example. He did not pretend to understand these
outsiders who tended and fed him, a stranger, as if he were
a blood relation. Of one thing only was he certain—here
in this Healing Hall they did good deeds.

Three days after beginning the work of orderly, Thirty-
nine went to Doctor Morland's office with the floor nurse's
request for a special drug. This, a perishable serum im-
ported from America, was kept in the electric refrigerator
and given out only by one of the physicians.

At the door, the youth halted abruptly. Inside the room
the three foreigners and as many Chinese were gathered
about the radio. Hu Ih-hseng was twisting the dial knob from
one station to another. When the clear, familiar voice of the
young woman announcer at Nanking failed to come through,
Hu moved his hands in a gesture of failure and exclaimed,
"Well, the Capital is gone—there's no doubt of that."

For a long moment those around him said nothing. Then
Miss Benton becoming conscious of the figure in the doorway
asked abruptly, "What is your business?"

San-djiu handed over the message, which in turn was
passed to Doctor Morland.

"I'll get it, Doctor," Hu Ih-hseng suggested. "I have a
dressing to do over in the wing." Then he added in Chinese,
"Li, come with me!"

As they went down the hall together, Thirty-nine asked
hesitantly, "Honorable Doctor, what of Nan Ching (Nanking)?"

"Captured like Shanghai and Soochow and all the other places. Where is our Army I wish to know?"

"And the Government?"

"Several days ago the Government left the city. It is said they are in Hankow." Handing over the small glass vial, he finished somberly, "Careful—do not drop that! If they close the Yangtze, Heaven alone knows whether we ever get more!"

The next evening at sunset a truck drove into the compound. Thirty-nine, waiting for a patient to finish a glass of fruit juice, was looking down from a window of the ward. There was something peculiar, he thought, about the general appearance of the machine; the top in particular was a mass of blackened holes of varying sizes. Slowly the wheels came to a stop. A door opened and a man crawled out from the driver's seat. With what seemed the greatest difficulty, he walked the few feet to the entrance steps, crumpled, and rolled over on his face.

The next minute the floor nurse called sharply, "Li, hurry! They need you downstairs."

As he reached there, the unconscious driver was already being carried inside, with Doctor Morland and Miss Benton in attendance. "Hu Ih-hseng wants you in the yard," directed a servant and there the youth ran.

After his previous experiences San-djiu had supposed himself hardened to gruesome sights, but as he helped unload that truck he felt a wild desire to retch a number of times. In it were thirty-two wounded soldiers, their bodies purple with cold, their wounds black from dried blood. How

so many could have been packed in so small a space seemed
incredible. Of the thirty-two, fourteen had died on the
way. That any of the others would live was doubtful indeed as their bodies were carried into the building. The
Red Cross driver who had rescued them from the battlefield
was among the dead, and his assistant, unconscious. A
wounded officer who also knew how to drive a car had
managed somehow to take the first motorist's place. With
two bullets in his left leg and a bayonet slash on a shoulder,
he had by some miracle of strength and will power brought
them to their goal.

The Hour of the Ox had come and gone before the last
soldier had been treated and placed on a clean cot-bed. Li
and the other orderly, having relieved night nurses for sur-
gical work, were still on duty. When the two physicians
came from the operating room, Thirty-nine watched them
move slowly down the hall. Hu Ih-hseng looked exhausted.
There was little doubt that his companion was in the same
condition, but for the moment weariness did not show on him.
From a set white face Meng Ih-hseng's dark eyes blazed.
Both men were sunk in silence, and at the end of the corridor the two parted without a word and went their separate
ways.

A little later in his own bed Thirty-nine heard a delirious
young soldier from a near-by room cry, "Ma! Ma!" in longing for his mother. The sound made the listener recall the
expression on Doctor Morland's face. Among all in the
hospital the American physician was known for calm, even
temper. Something out of the ordinary had been needed to

fire that one's anger to such heat. Pondering this, the youth fell asleep.

On the following morning details of what had happened to the Red Cross truck buzzed like angry bees about the hospital corridors. One soldier in less critical condition than the others had been able after treatment to give a brief account of the affair.

The machine serving as ambulance had been a long time reaching their sector of the battlefield. The driver and his assistant brought the gloomy information that the nearest First Aid Station had been demolished and the road to the Base Hospital blocked. There remained only one other possibility of medical assistance. On the north shore a good highway led directly to the Mission Hospital at Y——. The problem would be finding a ferry to take them across the Yangtze. How long so uncertain a journey might require no one could say. Crowding the vehicle would be bad for wounded men, but leaving them on the field meant certain death. As a result of this reasoning, twice the usual load of helpless occupants had been accommodated.

"Having that many in so small a space was enough to kill all," Hu Ih-hseng had interrupted.

"At first it was not too bad. Although no one could move, lying close together helped to keep us warm." For a moment or two pain sealed the speaker's lips. When he spoke again it was to say, "The river bank, our driver told us, was black with refugees. Finally, one boatman with two sons in the Army had pity, made room for our truck, and ferried us over safely. Not until we were on the great road did the trouble happen. Motors roared overhead and the next minute machine gun bullets tore through the roof. We could neither move nor see what was going on outside. For many the Wheel of Life abruptly stopped; for me it continued turning."

He breathed deeply, then went on to the end. "Soon after the airplane flew off the car stopped. Above the groans about me I could hear the driver's assistant cry, 'Help!'

"Our wounded captain heard it too. 'What do you want?' he called, and then a second time.

" 'My companion is dead,' came the answer, 'My arm! my arm—*ai!*'

"I saw the Captain struggle to free himself from the others. After that I knew nothing until they brought me into this building."

Receiving the account at secondhand from a servant, Sandjiu remarked, "That captain must be a brave man. One thing, though, I do not understand. Last night Meng Ih-hseng's temper was greatly fired. I myself saw it. Was one of the dead men his friend?"

"He had never seen them before. Beh Hsiao-je explained the affair to the nurse on the lower floor. Most nations of the world have an agreement in war not to harm hospitals or vehicles carrying wounded. That no mistakes are made such machines have the large healing cross on top and sides, like the one on our roof."

"Perhaps the 'dwarfs' do not know this law."

"Hsiao-je said the Japanese had signed the bond with the others."

Still puzzled, Thirty-nine turned away. The Lieutenant had once told him that Japan had broken all her contracts with China. Why then should anyone have expected this to be kept? In the suddenly increased demands of the day, troublesome questions were soon pushed from his mind.

There had been a full quota of patients in the hospital before the soldiers' arrival. With so many additional difficult cases to look after, the medical staff knew few idle moments.

San-djiu felt a real satisfaction in being around army men once more. Also, he could not help but relish his present position of authority when memory recalled the former days of teasing and bullying at soldiers' hands. The wounded men on their part sensed this orderly's interest in themselves and called for him constantly.

"Most countrymen dislike the military," commented Hu Ih-hseng one morning. "Why not you?"

"Since I was an infant I have known fellows like these," was the reply. Almost before he realized it the youth found himself talking freely about the Fort and his associations there.

Listening, the Chinese physician went on with the dressing of a wound. For some time he had been thinking seriously of joining the Army Medical Corps. Uncertainty about the troops' morale had kept him from doing so. In spite of a good deal of faith in the Generalissimo, lately the overwhelming accumulation of defeats had made Hu wonder if the Government were strong enough to last.

Since the Japanese now held both Nanking and Peiping, in time they would certainly seize the railroad between the two. Y—— was an essential link in the chain of communications. How long a time might elapse before the city was taken was a problem to be solved only by the invaders. When that day came, there would be no place for him here even if the Americans managed to keep the hospital open. He was a physician concerned with the business of saving life, but first he was a Chinese. To try to work with these devils who were engulfing China in blood and suffering was beyond his nature. Already there was talk of *Ih Yung Chün* (Righteous Fighters—guerrillas) forming a band in the hills in advance of the expected invasion. The experience of cities on the southern bank of the Yangtze had, at least, taught men to be forehanded. If necessary he would serve as doctor for that group of patriots.

Whatever he did, though, it might be good to have young Li as helper. The youth was not likely ever to have the book knowledge required of graduate nurses, but in practical work he might prove better than many from the schools. A common fault of orderlies was roughness in handling patients; perhaps caring for the old man had helped to make this one gentle. The soldiers preferred him to a nurse —a high compliment indeed. Today he would show the other how to do simple bandaging and give a hypodermic.

Two of the wounded had died since arrival. Most of the others would doubtless recover; the Captain alone failed to respond to good care and treatment. A transfusion of blood might work wonders, but the patient had the rare type, Number 1, that was hard to match. Already all hospital workers except the servants had been tested; since Chinese generally had a deep-rooted aversion to such foreign practices, Doctor Morland had not yet bothered these helpers.

So far, Li's age had eliminated him. On entering the hospital service, the youth had been given a thorough physical examination. He was as large and strong as many a man, but Western medical theory disapproved of growing youths as blood donors. If the Captain, though, did not soon show some sign of improvement, all objections to testing servants and Li would have to be overruled.

Within the next forty-eight hours the patient grew steadily weaker. Meeting Li in the laboratory, Hu Ih-hseng reached a quick decision. "Come here," he said. "I want to type your blood."

With mental reservations San-djiu held out his arm for the blood to be extracted. When this was done the physician went efficiently through the necessary processes with test tubes, slides, and microscope. Hu Doctor looked away from the results and staring at the youth murmured, "Too hard to believe!"

"What, Honorable Doctor?"

"That you have such blood. Wait here a minute!" At once the speaker disappeared.

Alone, Thirty-nine moved about the small room with its strange equipment. The nurse who had sent him here with a specimen would scold about the prolonged absence if the doctor did not soon return. He stood by the microscope and, leaning down with hands clasped behind him, squinted in the eyepiece. It was said this foreign machine made things hundreds of times larger. He himself could see nothing but a round white space. No one ever touched the article, he had been warned, except the two physicians, and perhaps their eyes had something his lacked.

In the meantime Hu Ih-hseng had gone to Doctor Morland's office and related the findings. "But Hu, the fellow will not be sixteen for another month, if the age given us was correct," Meng Ih-hseng said, then paused, frowning thoughtfully.

"That he should have Number 1 is the surprise; though, of course, one can never tell where it may be found."

"Well, Doctor, the Captain is your patient, not mine."

"What does the boy say?"

"I have not yet asked him. He's still in the laboratory."

Together they went there. "Li," began Doctor Morland, "you have an unusual kind of blood."

"Is it bad, Meng Ih-hseng?"

The American smiled. "No, very good! It might help to save a life."

Thirty-nine's eyebrows lifted. Sometimes these healers talked in riddles. "How, Honorable Doctor?"

"Suppose we asked you to give some away?"

"My blood? What would I do without it?"

"You would probably not know it was gone."

San-djiu was silent. This was the first idea of the foreigners he had ever questioned. His ancestors had given him this blood, and they undoubtedly expected him to hold onto it. When the time came to die, how could such an affair be explained to them? It was clear, though, that these two men who had done so much for him and Lao To hoped for his agreement to their plan. Finally he said, "Can do!" then added, "better it is we do not tell Old Head."

No more time was lost. They were soon at the Captain's bedside with the transfusion in process. At the end, a nurse appeared with a pot of hot tea. "Li, drink this," Doctor Morland ordered. "After you have rested here for a little, go to your own bed and stay there this afternoon. The cook will send you a tray of food. Eat all of it, then sleep."

Awaking several hours later, Thirty-nine admitted to himself that he felt none the worse for the transfusion. There had not even been a shrinking of his veins—a result that anyone might have expected. The foreign method of taking blood from one man and putting it into another still made him shiver, but only the foolish worried about what was already past. Lao To need not know of the affair; and perhaps with the passing of years, even the ancestral spirits would forget.

Next morning as the young orderly went on duty, Doctor Morland halted him in the corridor. "Li, the Captain is better," he said. "The day I met you in that village was one of good fortune for him—and for us. You do your work well."

San-djiu's eyes lighted at these expressions of approval. Murmuring unworthiness, he bowed himself away. At least the latter part of the commendation could be shared with Lao To, and this was done at the first opportunity.

CHAPTER IX

"The Raven, Though Washed and Powdered, Still Remains Black"

OLD HEAD, whose every thought was connected with his grandson, lived for their brief moments together. At such times, Li Thirty-nine told him bits of gossip about other patients or gave him news of the outside world. What interested the grandfather more than anything else, naturally, was hearing about the other's work. Both the physicians had spoken kindly of the youth—the Chinese, called Hu, with particular concern.

Deep in his own heart, Lao To had the feeling that life for him would not last very much longer. Through the given years he had tried to do the best possible for his family. Now body and mind were tired, and soon the time would come to join the ancestors. Leaving San-djiu had been the only worry. Each day, however, as the elder became more fully aware of the boy's ability to take care of himself, personal responsibility seemed to lessen. "In the child you can tell the man," was an old saying, which in their own case had been proved true indeed.

While Old Head lay marooned on the small island of peace that was his hospital bed, the world immediately outside was slipping into chaos. Without glimpsing a single enemy soldier, Y—— was beginning to experience some of the horrors of war.

Recently, planes had flown over the city twice at night and dropped incendiary bombs. One of these, surprisingly enough, had hit its target accurately, for the railroad station had been seriously damaged. The second choice for destruction, the Government High School, had escaped. The bomb had exploded in a marsh near the building and gradually died out. In the vicinity of the school a lone farm wife caring for a sick child at midnight had seen a small light moving about the institution just before the airplane could be heard. Her testimony led local officials to believe that someone was signaling the enemy flyers.

Until the beginning of the conflict, there had been a sizable community of Japanese within the city. Promptly with the outbreak of hostilities they had left on trains bound for the Coast. It was difficult to think that a Chinese citizen might have been guilty of this treachery, but as a precaution several questionable characters were arrested and confined

to the *Ya-men* (court and prison). Although investigation
failed to settle blame on any one of these, the court decided
to hold them for a time. With this attended to and enemy
nationals already eliminated, suspicion fell next on the
Refugee Camp.

In the days immediately following the fall of Nanking,
terrified civilians had crowded all highways leading west.
A hundred or two falling away from the fleeing mob like
grains of sand from an overloaded cart had been swept
slowly northward and into the haven of Y——. All refugee
groups were accompanied by the fearful specter of disease
epidemics, and city officials now consulted Doctor Morland
about handling the unhappy visitors. On arrival they had
settled at random wherever overhanging eaves or covered
alleyways seemed to offer some protection from winter
weather. The physician immediately suggested establishing
them in a temporary village of mat sheds on the outskirts
of the larger community. There a degree of sanitation impossible in the city proper might be maintained. The hospital staff would supervise this and look after general medical
needs, he promised, if some benevolent organization would
help supply food. In a remarkably short time the mush-
room-like village began to function.

The inhabitants had originally come from every class in
life, but war had forced them all to the same level of existence. Among these, women, the aged, and children pre-
dominated. Most able-bodied men had remained in hide-
outs near their homes hoping to return to fields and trades
when the smoke of battle cleared.

In spite of the help from outside, misery dwelt within the mat sheds. In flight, families had been torn apart. There were mothers without children and children without parents. Many older sons and brothers had been among the troops protecting Nanking, and of them the refugees dared not even think. With the usual speed of bad news, rumors of atrocities to captured soldiers had overtaken the fleeing relatives on the road. From then on all hope for their young men had died; that fathers and husbands still remained in the path of the enemy made each woman's mind desperate with anxiety. Occasionally someone asked with stiff lips for news from the Front. When nothing definite was forthcoming, she managed in spite of heartbreak to murmur polite thanks. Having lost everything else, these people still held on to courtesy, gratitude, and a degree of cheerfulness.

On his trip to the Refugee Camp with Hu Ih-hseng, Sandjiu, waiting while the doctor talked with a patient, became interested in the people about him. A few individuals overwhelmed by grief wrapped themselves in silent loneliness and inactivity, but most were busy. It was amazing how much work the women, in particular, seemed to find at hand. Meng Si-mu had said that they begged her constantly for mending and sewing materials. "Foreign Mistress, if our hands have something to do we can better endure trouble," a middle-aged housewife had insisted. As a result of this plea, Mrs. Morland was now holding classes in handicrafts twice a week. At present this provided occupation; in the future, such skills might help them earn a livelihood.

She was showing the other how to knit.

On the ground a few feet away from Thirty-nine a small maid of about ten in age leaned toward one several years younger. In the larger one's hands were a half-dozen frayed strands of wool and two badly burnt foreign match-sticks. With this strange equipment she was showing the other how to knit. Gradually the bits of wool thread became a rough two-inch square of material. As soon as this was finished, the child ripped it apart. "Now, Me-me (Small Sister)," she said, "you do it."

A second time the performance was repeated, then the younger wearied of the work. "I do not want to knit," she whimpered. "I want Mother."

"Do not cry, Me-me," her sister chided gravely. "Soon we shall eat. Today you may drink my share of the bean milk with the sugar in it, but first you must knit again. When Mother comes, she will see you have not forgotten her teaching."

San-djiu, smiling to himself over the determination of this small girl-child, became conscious of Hu Ih-hseng beside him. Surprisingly the Chinese physician reached in the pocket of his foreign suit, pulled out two matches, lit them for a second, then scratched off the charred ends. Walking over to the children, he said in all seriousness, "Je-je (Big Sister), these will make better needles than yours." As the child glanced up timidly to thank him, he added, "When your parents come they will be proud of you."

Starting away from the village, San-djiu asked curiously, "Where are their parents?"

"No one knows. They are alone in the camp."

A priest with an acolyte carrying a basket of grain for the refugees now passed them. Still thinking about the children, San-djiu looked up in time to catch only a side view of these pedestrians, but there was something vaguely familiar about one.

Noticing his interest, the physician also looked back. "It is past time," he said, "for the Temple Abbot to contribute something to the camp. His establishment is a wealthy one, and you can be certain the storehouses are stocked with food."

The very next day court officials sent representatives to question the occupants of the mat sheds. Then erecting a spiked bamboo fence about the community, they placed a guard at the entrance.

In the hospital this move was widely discussed. Most Chinese thought it the wise thing to do. The two foreign women disagreed. San-djiu, wheeling a patient into a sunny corridor, overheard Beh Hsiao-je, who was given to frank speech, say to a Chinese nurse, "Why not ask the farm wife if she noticed any strangers that day? What do those poor fleeing-trouble-people in the camp know of the affair? I realize that the guard at the gate does only his duty. Seeing him, though, the refugees must feel like criminals wearing cangues."

"But, Beh Hsiao-je, the next day officials questioned the woman," replied the nurse. "Many people pass her house and she was too busy with the sick child to pay much attention. She remembered going outside only once, at sundown.

This was to collect garments from the poles where they had been put to dry. One thing she recalled—a farmer with a donkey, for the beast was lame. There were also some load-bearers, a Buddhist priest, and a boy riding a *shui-niu*, so she thought, but these might have been seen the day before. Moreover, this was long before twelve o'clock when she saw that light."

"What about the railroad station?" Mrs. Morland's voice now asked.

Thirty-nine had to think a little about this question. Meng Si-mu's Chinese was still difficult for him to understand. She did not speak the language so well as Beh Hsiao-je or the Doctor.

"Meng Si-mu," the nurse explained, "the man in charge said there had been a great many travelers for the evening train: perhaps thirty young people going out to a village for a patriotic meeting, several well-to-do families on the way to a wedding, and as usual a great many laborers. Who else, he could not say. It was his business to sell tickets and watch that no one stepped in front of the *ho-chae* (fire-cart). When the train left he remembered seeing some Boy Scouts and a priest among others still on the platform— and that was all. If the officials could find the guilty wretch, nothing would please him better, the stationmaster assured them. Trying to work in a wrecked building was no easy affair."

Readjusting pillows for his patient in the sunny corridor, Thirty-nine found himself concentrating on what he had just heard. The nurse had used the foreign way of telling hours.

Twelve o'clock probably meant in the Hour of the Rat. Suddenly with blinding clarity there now came to him what he must do.

As soon as his regular two-hour period of freedom arrived, the youth went on the street and made directly for the Buddhist Temple. Mingling with a family group he entered the building and found a shadowy corner in the main hall. There squatting against the wall, with his eyes narrowed to slits, he gave an appearance of one lost in meditation. For the next half hour the watcher stayed there, missing no single detail of what went on. After a time, doubts began to assail his mind—perhaps the idea of coming here had been nonsense. A group of pilgrims entered noisily, and, a moment later, excitement surged in his veins. For another ten minutes, Thirty-nine sat motionless in the darkened corner and fixed attention on the object of his visit. Then slipping unobtrusively away, he hurried back to the hospital.

For once, thanks to Good Fortune, Hu Ih-hseng was in his office and alone. "Honorable Doctor," San-djiu began without further delay, "I think I have found the one they seek."

The Chinese physician looked up in surprise. "You— what is this?" came the question.

"It is a long story and perhaps the time is not enough ——"

Doctor Morland now came in, swinging a stethoscope and interrupted, "What story?"

"There is a Japanese in the Buddhist Temple."

"How do you know?" asked Hu Ih-hseng.

Thirty-nine hunted for words. "When my grandfather and I were journeying here, we stopped one night at a temple in the country. The next morning I talked with one of their priests. Afterwards I could not forget this. I . . ."

"What did he say?" broke in Doctor Morland.

"Nothing important, but something about him troubled me. Yesterday, returning from the camp with Hu Ih-hseng, we passed a priest and a helper. I thought I had seen the priest before."

"So that is why you looked back?" Hu Doctor asked.

Li nodded. "Then today I overheard a nurse telling Beh Hsiao-je and Meng Si-mu what the farm wife and the man at the railroad had said to officials. Each one had mentioned a Buddhist priest among the people seen."

"Is it strange for a Buddhist priest to be in a crowd?"

"No, but ——"

"Go on, Li," urged Doctor Morland.

"There were too many Buddhist priests inside my head," Thirty-nine replied with an unexpected grin. "Late this afternoon I went to the Temple. In time I saw the one we had passed yesterday. He was the same man who had talked to me in the country."

Again Hu Ih-hseng interrupted, "Some priests wander from one temple to another."

"That did not trouble me, Doctor, it was the way this fellow spoke. I knew he was a Japanese."

"How?"

"Those 'dwarfs' who came on the ships, even the one who spoke a little Chinese, did strange things with their mouths.

I mentioned it to the Lieutenant, and he said all Nipponese talked that way."

"And does this priest do the same?"

"Only when he forgets. For that reason, in the country temple I could not tell what troubled me. Today, I watched him talk to pilgrims. He speaks Chinese well, but three times his lips forgot to do what he had told them!"

"You think that the other priests would not see this for themselves?" Hu Ih-hseng asked skeptically.

Thirty-nine shrugged his shoulders in answer.

Doctor Morland slipped into the breach. "Hu, suppose you go over there with Li and see for yourself. If true, I will report to the *Ya-men* at once."

There were not many people coming and going now on the steps that led into the Temple's main hall, so there was no opportunity of mingling with a crowd. To make this visit seem natural, Hu Ih-hseng led San-djiu about, much as if he were a teacher explaining Buddhism to an inquiring student. Before each of the huge gilt-encrusted images representing Buddhist deities, they paused for a brief discussion. Priests moved in leisurely fashion past them and after one glance at the physician's foreign clothes paid no more attention.

Suddenly Thirty-nine stiffened and without turning his head murmured, "Careful, that short one to the left of the Great Buddha!"

While the youth continued to stare at the image immediately before him, Hu Ih-hseng strolled casually in the direction indicated and engaged the priest in conversation.

Later rejoining Young Li, the doctor continued his pretense at instruction. Gradually they worked their way back to the entrance and there paused to admire the frieze of sacred animals.

As his gaze descended from wall to floor, San-djiu found himself looking straight into the face of the suspected priest, who had also managed to reach the doorway. For a long breath the two exchanged glances, then the youth followed Hu Ih-hseng down the steps. At the bottom he could not resist a backward look. Outlined in the dim light of a ceiling lantern, this questionable representative of Buddha was standing exactly where they had left him.

Back with Doctor Morland, Hu said, "Li is right. When that fellow forgets, his lips narrow and words come out like a snake's hiss."

"Of course, it might be possible for a Chinese to have such a mannerism," suggested the American.

"Yes, that is why I doubted when Li told us."

"Then why are you so certain now?"

"Two Japanese attended the same medical school in America where I was. They had difficulty with the English sound, 'l,' as we sometimes do with the English, 'r.' Tonight I put questions that made him use the 'l' sounds in our own tongue. He stumbled badly."

"Then there is no more time to be lost." Doctor Morland reached for his hat and coat. "If I am not here within an hour, that soldier whose arm was amputated gets a hypodermic at bedtime." He turned to San-djiu. "Tell the floor nurse you are going out with me—and hurry."

At the *Ya-men,* they were promptly ushered inside. As Doctor Morland discussed the affair with the Hsien Chang (official), Li stood looking around. At the hospital he had become used to the fabulous foreign comforts. In this reception hall, however, the wall scrolls and tall porcelain jars that served as decoration were treasures such as the country boy had never glimpsed. Even in his ignorance he sensed the wealth and social position such furnishings expressed.

Suddenly Doctor Morland addressed him. "Li, His Excellency wishes you to go with two of the guards to arrest this fellow."

San-djiu's heart thudded. Like most civilians he had a healthy fear of courts and those who served in them. The thought of going with two "Dog-legs" (a common name for *Ya-men* runners) to arrest that Japanese was frightening. He glanced unhappily at Doctor Morland and at once the other's quiet voice reassured him. "Lay down your heart! All you need do is to point out the man, then go back to the hospital. His Excellency has already explained this."

Following the guards through dark streets to the Temple, Young Li's uneasiness lessened. The two asked him an occasional question, but most of their conversation was limited to discussion of food, wages, and family affairs. In spite of their positions it was evident that *Ya-men* guards were just like other men.

At the Temple, frightened priests led the three to the Abbot. That dignitary received them coldly, and breaking the seal on the official paper, read the contents with deliberation. Finally he said with a frown, "Does the Hsien Chang consider it good custom to take innocent priests from temples and imprison them?" Then as if expecting no reply, he went on, "True, the man you seek has been here only a few days more than a moon, but that he is Japanese is nonsense.

"Tell the new one to come to me here," he ordered the young priest who stood at his elbow. This messenger was gone a long time. When he returned it was with two others of his profession. Neither of these was the man desired.

"Honorable Sir Abbot," the young priest reported fearfully, "we have searched the halls and courts, but the man you wish cannot be found."

Satisfied assurance suddenly faded from the Abbot's face. He rose and said to the guards, "Come with me! I myself will take you through our buildings."

When they had finished, Thirty-nine felt that there was nothing left for him to learn about a Buddhist temple; but what the priest had first reported was true—their quarry was gone. Having missed no likely hiding place, the guards returned at once to the Ya-men and San-djiu hurried back to the hospital.

There he reported the failure.

"So that fellow is free to do more damage," Hu Ih-hseng exclaimed, disgusted.

"They may still pick him up in the city," suggested Doctor Morland. "Not many men have heads shaven so close as priests. I suppose, though, he uses other disguises at will." The American turned suddenly to Li. "Even if they do not find him, your work was good. Although the guards were sent to make the arrest, the Hsien Chang doubted that the fellow was Japanese. This disappearance should settle the question."

"I am most unworthy!" San-djiu replied, then said hesitantly, "Had I been more careful, tonight he might not have seen me."

"Why should the priest have guessed your thoughts?" Hu Ih-hseng wanted to know.

"Perhaps he had a strange feeling, Honorable Doctor."

"A hunch," Meng Ih-hseng suggested in English, with a smile.

"What, Sir?"

"A 'hunch' is what they say in America."

"Hun-che," repeated Young Li, "hun-che." This was another English word to add to the nine or ten already learned.

"Not bad," teased the foreigner.

The Chinese physician rose wearily and stretching put an end to the others' language lesson. "I gave your patient his hypodermic, Doctor; now I shall go to sleep." Changing swiftly to Chinese speech, he said half to himself, "Railroad stations, schools, hospitals—everywhere they bomb these first. I wish we knew where that priest is tonight." Yawning, he walked away and Thirty-nine followed, but not before he had seen a thoughtful expression grow in Doctor Morland's eyes.

Whether the spy succeeded that night in again signaling planes, no one ever discovered. For the third time bombs fell on Y——, but if meant for the Mission property or anywhere else of importance they went wide of the mark. Instead, the missiles landed some distance away in one of the city's poorest residential sections. The railroad station had, of course, been a fair military target, but a good reason for the last attack or the previous attempt on the High School was hard to find. Through painful experience China was learning that the Japanese always did the unexpected. From the beginning they had seemed to carry out an incomprehensible plan of destruction with regard to cultural institutions. Whether this had been the purpose at Y——, or whether the light bombings were merely a softening-up process before invasions, the victims had no way of knowing.

For several hours fires raged in the stricken quarter. The youth organizations that in the recent training courses had played at rescue work now found themselves doing so in earnest.

Startled out of sound sleep by the explosions, Hu Ih-hseng, two nurses, and Thirty-nine commandeered the battered Red Cross truck and made their way to the scene of disaster. Those found with minor injuries were given First Aid on the spot. More serious cases were put into the machine and carried to the hospital.

There everyone was on duty. With rooms and wards already filled to normal capacity, space had to be made for extra cots and pallets. Many of these overflowed into corridors, and through the night, staff and servants labored to meet the demands of the new situation.

By daybreak fires burned low and the streets of humble homes were now but charred and smoking ruins. In the gray hour of winter dawning, the uninjured sat wailing beside their dead or clustered in the hospital gateway patiently awaiting word of relatives inside.

In the first lull after activity, San-djiu stared amazed at his own image in the washroom mirror. Front hair was scorched and on one cheek a burn stood out angrily from streaks and smears of black. His hands were badly scratched and the white uniform, now discolored from soot, bore several small burned holes. Hu Ih-hseng and the nurses must be in the same condition, he told himself, but in the desperate work of salvaging lives all had been unconscious of their own bodies and of each other's.

Earlier there had been no time for contemplative thought, but now the youth wondered what part the missing priest had played in tonight's affair. It was discouraging to think that the latest bombing might not have occurred had the fellow been behind bars in the *Ya-men*. Where was he at present and in what disguise? Few Buddhist priests were supposed to have heads full of brains, but the Japanese having fooled them so easily could doubtless fool others. As long as that one was free, he would always be a menace.

Ten days had passed since the bombing and most of the injured civilians had recovered sufficiently to return home. One by one the wounded soldiers also were improving; several were now permitted to walk about corridors. The Captain had progressed to a wheel chair, and hospital routine was swiftly returning to normalcy.

At the Refugee Camp there was no longer a guard. Evidently the disappearance of the priest had settled the last doubt in official minds about his nationality, and lifted suspicion from everyone else.

In the city proper, inhabitants went about their daily tasks with usual diligence. Business men unable either to buy or sell at the Coast sucked in their lips and figured other ways of making income. If these particular citizens felt the war closing like a net about them, that was not true of the majority. In an atmosphere of comparative peace betrothals were arranged; children went gaily to and from schools; births and deaths occurred with unexciting regularity.

The feeling of security, however, existed only on the surface, for the authorities were grave with concern. Word had arrived that the enemy was now north of the Yangtze. Advancing along the railroad, the invaders were slowly but surely cutting a swathe of victory a *li* in width on either side. When massed armies at Shanghai and Nanking had failed to stop the Japanese, the city's protectors knew their own cause was hopeless.

One night after evening rice, Hu Ih-hseng sent for San-djiu. "At present Wei Orderly will relieve on your floor," he announced; "you and I have other affairs."

A few minutes later in the small hospital car, they moved swiftly along the highway leading south. After fifteen or twenty minutes of steady driving, the physician parked the machine in a lonely spot and the two got out. Thirty-nine looked around. With the moon hidden behind clouds, very little of the countryside could be seen, but even that was strange to him. Since being appointed orderly, he had on several occasions accompanied one of the doctors on visits to distant patients, but never before in this locality.

Shielding a flash light with both hands, Hu Ih-hseng focused it on the ground about him. Then returning the darkened torch to his pocket, he said, "Here it is—this field path to the right. Now, let us hurry!"

To make haste on a strange path at night was no easy matter. It would have been much simpler with the help of the light, Thirty-nine told himself, but he supposed Hu Doctor had some good reason for not using the foreign object.

After a time they came out on a country road. At the same moment a man stepped from the shadows. The unexpected encounter here where not even the dark outlines of a house were visible startled the youth badly, but his companion showed no sign of surprise. "National Salvation!" he murmured in greeting the stranger.

"National Salvation!" came the response. "You are the Honorable Doctor named Hu?"

"Not wrong."

"This other?"

"My assistant."

"Please follow me."

The next moment they left the level land and began to climb. Footing became constantly more difficult. The leader, evidently familiar with the terrain, made good headway; but physician and orderly, stumbling over loose roots and stones, had all they could do to keep from falling.

Later a second man, appearing as quietly as the first, joined them and helped break a path through tangled underbrush. In the side of the hill an entrance swung open to receive the newcomers. It was as swiftly closed upon their heels. A single flickering candle served to light the large cave into which they had now come. The place seemed full of men, though which of these were real and which oversized shadows on the walls San-djiu at first had difficulty in deciding. The physician's attention was promptly directed to three figures on the floor, and for the next hour or so the two from the hospital were kept busy dressing wounds.

Not until Hu Ih-hseng was once more driving along the homeward stretch to Y—— did he offer his companion an explanation of this strange visit.

"Li," he began, "when that call came, I had to have a trustworthy assistant. You were chosen because you work well and talk little. What you saw tonight, or may see in the future, must be locked in memory. If anyone else asks where we went, answer, 'To see an injured farmer!'"

Thirty-nine's interest, which had been racing along with this account, halted abruptly at the last statement. He had never known people to be so careful of truth as those on the medical staff. They permitted no worker to use the common phrase, "*Ch'a puh do*," (lacks not much, almost) about any duty however small. When a patient was ordered a foreign teaspoonful of medicine, a teaspoonful was administered, not one drop more or less. Most Chinese accustomed to centuries of adapting themselves to all sorts of

difficult situations were seldom painfully exact.   Yet Hu Ih-
hseng was now directing him to tell what seemed false.

As if sensing this questioning, the physician continued,
"That is truer than you think.   One of those wounded men
was a farmer."

"Their knives and guns made them look like bandits."

"Truly not!   They are Righteous Fighters.   Merchants,
students, artisans, farmers—all are sworn to fight until Nippon is defeated.   Their leader, my friend, is an engineer."

"The enemy has not yet come here.   How then were
those men hurt?"

"Each night they go secretly to map the land along railroad, streams, and highways—thus is gained knowledge for
use after invasion.   Last night the band went farther south
than usual and unexpectedly met a Japanese scouting party.
Fortunately the 'dwarfs' were equally surprised by the meeting; otherwise we should have had to care for more than
three wounded.   Though poorly armed our men killed two
of the invaders and injured others, so my friend told me."

San-djiu was stirred by admiration.   This was the sort
of resistance he and Hsiao Pan had discussed.   Here at
last were men not waiting for trouble, but actually preparing
against it.   "Do all the Righteous Fighters live in the cave?"
he asked.

"Certainly not!   That is their meeting place at night.   In
the daylight they go quietly about regular business.   After
evening rice even their own families know nothing about
them."

Ai, what an affair! thought the youth.   In the future each man passed on the street would set him to wondering. "Some day I myself may join them," he suddenly volunteered.

"Perhaps we shall go together," Hu Ih-hseng remarked, then lapsed into silence for the rest of the drive.

CHAPTER X

"When the Boat Is in Midstream It Is Too Late to Mend the Leak"

AS THEY entered the hospital on their return from the camp, Doctor Morland emerged from his office. By the manner in which the two physicians exchanged glances, it was easy to see that they shared an understanding of this affair. The next instant the American turned to San-djiu and said gravely, "Li, your grandfather is much worse."

Assaulted by fear the youth stood still. From a dry throat he managed to protest, "But, Meng Ih-hseng, he was better, not so?"

"So we thought. Sometimes, though, when old people have pneumonia other trouble follows the disease. Your grandfather has a pleural abscess."

"What is that?"

"A sore in here." The physician placed his finger in the right location on Thirty-nine's chest.

"Some get better, Honorable Doctor, not so?"

Doctor Morland hesitated and Hu Ih-hseng stared at the floor. "Some, Li, but your Old One's heart is weak. That he lived through the pneumonia is surprising."

San-djiu stood there trying to accept what had just been said. Then Lao To was going to die—and soon.

Doctor Morland's next words fell faintly on his ears. "In English, Li, we have a wise saying, 'While there is life, there is hope.' Naturally Hu Ih-hseng and I will do everything we can for your grandfather, but I wished you to know how ill he is. An order shall be given the floor nurse to let you be with him as much as possible."

"At present may I go see him?"

"Certainly."

Later in the quiet darkness of his own room, Thirty-nine threw himself face downward on the bed. Lao To had been asleep and the grandson had come away without disturbing him. The elder had lived many years and like all men must die some day, he knew, but the knowledge did nothing to lessen grief. Tears suddenly scalded his eyelids. If Old Head died, he himself would be alone, the only one left of all their family.

When the first wave of emotion had passed, memory reminded him of the English words Doctor Morland had translated into Chinese. Since Grandfather was still alive, they could hope for recovery. Things always seemed worse at night; perhaps in the morning news would be better.

But the report the next day was even graver, and by the end of the week Lao To had gone to join the ancestors. Once or twice in those last days the old man rallied to find San-djiu at the bedside. The patient's words coming with great effort were few and disconnected. For the most part he lay silent with frail, toil-worn fingers clinging to his grandson's strong hand. This contact seemed to give him satisfaction, and it was the last thing that he knew.

In the period that followed, Li was only dimly aware of all the kindness received from foreigners and Chinese alike throughout the institution. Both physicians had offered to help pay funeral expenses, but pride had made him refuse. No matter how wretched their circumstances in life, the men of his race looked forward to decent burial. Sons and daughters who could afford to do so presented their aged parents with coffins long before Death arrived. For the wealthy these great boxes of thick, sweet-smelling lumber were beautifully lacquered and decorated. For the poor the satin finish of plain, unvarnished wood offered the only adornment. But wherever given, the objects brought contentment to recipients and were frequently placed prominently among the furnishings of the home. There with quiet pride owners showed them to guests or watched while children of the household climbed in and out at play. Lao To had asked little enough of life; in death he should fittingly go to his ancestors, the grandson determined.

Even after the journeying there had been some silver left from the boat sale. The Japanese objects given him by the Lieutenant would bring something more. Articles made in Japan were being boycotted; but if no merchant would take them, some pawnbroker would. If the amounts were still not enough, then he would borrow the rest from Meng Ih-hseng and ask to have it taken from wages. Previously the elder's expenses, though moderate indeed, had taken most of the small salary paid an orderly; now that sum could be used for this equally important purpose. To his great relief a loan did not become necessary, and at a suitable date Old Head was laid to rest in dignity.

While the bereaved youth was trying to overcome sorrow by work, the Japanese were continuing their advance northward. It was now the first week in February, and the Chinese New Year had come and gone. With the authorities following the foreign calendar and tradition demanding that the ancient Chinese one be observed, citizens were at a loss which to celebrate. Also, war and the approaching threat to Y—— had dampened the usual festive spirit. Only a few stubborn souls had insisted on doing what had always been done. When it was possible to hear the rumble of distant guns and the constant whirring of airplanes immediately overhead, any one of which might drop more bombs, the more serious minded citizen lost interest in feasts.

Each day brought the enemy nearer, and rapid changes began to take place in the community. Officials, with records packed, prepared to leave on short notice. Merchants took all stocks of value and removed them to rural safety zones. Most wealthy men had already boarded up houses and taken families and possessions elsewhere.

The great mass of citizens, clinging to their homes and unable to afford even the shortest vacation from daily work, continued with routine duties. Most of these regardless of fears and warnings would wait until the moment of invasion arrived before even considering flight. Others, a small minority, would stay on and try to come to terms with their conquerors.

The Refugee Camp had already been told of the coming danger and its destitute occupants advised to move on. No longer could these fleeing-trouble-people hope to return home soon, for the Japanese had blocked the roads leading south. Instead, one small group after another departed from the mat shed village and started west across the countryside. Mechanically they moved forward without hope of food or shelter on the way, possessing neither a goal nor means of support to help them reach one.

At the hospital, the staff was engrossed with its own worries. In the invaded cities the enemy had destroyed foreign hospitals by a method which was becoming known as, "Sorry —a mistake!" or had adapted the institutions to their own purposes.

The Hospital Board in the United States had left the final decision concerning this one in Doctor Morland's hands. He was aware that destruction of the property might occur whether the establishment was functioning or not, and noth-

ing could be done about the matter. For him staying on
or going elsewhere was the real question.

Today China offered a thousand opportunities to every
available physician. It seemed likely that better medical
service might be rendered on a battle front or in unoccupied territory than in a city that the Japanese would soon
hold. In Free China all personal dealings with the conquerors could be avoided—a strong temptation, indeed,
for their treatment of Chinese civilians in this conflict made
him burn with fury. Yet, if open, the hospital and compound flying the Stars and Stripes might on the day of invasion provide the only refuge in Y—— for hundreds of
Chinese patients and friends. And for that possibility he
was willing to put up with a great deal personally at the
enemy's hands. Stronger than anything else, perhaps, was a
feeling of obligation. The thought that his own great country, together with the other democracies, was supplying Japan
with her war munitions made him bitterly unhappy. In so
far as one man's services could help to counteract this traffic,
he would give them without stint.

Calling a meeting of staff and servants, the doctor in-
formed them of his wish to keep the institution running. Mrs.
Morland and Miss Benton at once agreed with this plan.
"At present Japan would be foolish to harm Americans,"
Beh Hsiao-je continued. "Even *her* generals must be satis-
fied with one war at a time."

"Of course, they have destroyed some foreign property
in other cities," Hu Ih-hseng interrupted quietly; "also, do

not forget they sank the American gunboat, *Panay*, and shot the British Ambassador."

"Perhaps those were accidents," ventured Mrs. Morland.

"Perhaps!" Hu Ih-hseng admitted with a half smile.

Doctor Morland now spoke again. "Many patients are anxious to join their families. Today all able to be moved shall do so. Until the Captain and the remaining soldiers leave day after tomorrow, we can use the truck for this purpose. Only the few very ill cases need remain. Beh Hsiao-je, Meng Si-mu, and I can take care of them. For a time it would be wise for all Chinese helpers to seek safety elsewhere."

Surprised murmurs greeted this statement. A nurse was the first to volunteer remaining. "I am the only one alive in all our family," he said. "What I do is my own affair; I will stay."

"Someone must be at the entrance," said the old gateman. "Does Meng Ih-hseng think the Japanese would respect a foreigner who did such work?"

The physician had his own ideas about who should receive the enemy when the time came, but he accepted this offer courteously.

The chief cook asked, "Food—what of that?"

"Before you leave see that we have a plentiful supply," Doctor Morland replied. "If necessary, Meng Si-mu can prepare more."

Cook stared aghast, his usually squinting eyes forced wide open. The idea of Foreign Mistress taking over the kitchen

was too much to bear. For a woman she had many virtues, but
the two of them seldom agreed on the way to do his work.

"Honorable Doctor, I myself—no other—will prepare the
food in this building," he declared stubbornly. "Moreover,
my family dwells in a village west a hundred *li*." To himself he added, "And if one of those short-legged devils both-
ers me, I will slit his neck like a fowl's for stuffing." This
very day every kitchen knife should be freshly sharpened,
was the next decision. To have a little poison handy might
also be a good idea—cooks had unusual opportunities. He
would naturally not mention such plans to the foreigners.
Meng Ih-hseng, for instance, spent most of his time cutting
sick men open but the physician would doubtless object to
hurrying a well man, even a Japanese, into the spirit world.
After ten years of cooking for these foreigners, he still did
not understand them.

An upsetting thought suddenly occurred to him: how
could anyone cook without someone to prepare vegetables and
wash dishes? Not a single kitchen helper had yet opened
his mouth. And he himself had gotten all of them their
jobs. Chang, the fellow standing next, had even been brought
the long distance from the home village, a hundred *li* away
to fill this desirable place in a foreigner's kitchen. And
such was his gratitude! Suddenly a rough prod in the ribs
reminded Chang where duty lay. Thus coerced, the assistant did not even think of disobedience. Having already
made a swift and pleasant journey home, his mind turned
and retraced its way unhappily to the work in hand. Like

a prisoner reading his own sentence Chang announced timidly, "I too stay here."

The gardener and still another servant added their names.
As if trying to avoid influencing others, Hu Ih-hseng was
among the last.

"But Hu," Doctor Morland protested, then left the speech
unfinished. Whatever there was to say would apparently be
held for a more private moment.

Li had listened quietly to the whole affair. Until Hu Ih-
hseng spoke, his own mind had not been settled about the
matter. True, there was no family for him to worry about.
He did not, however, wish to meet the enemy again, even
in an American hospital. Now, with Lao To gone, escaping westward would be simple. But the Chinese physician
whose saliva also flowed bitter at the thought of them, had
just offered to stay. Moreover, the three foreigners could
certainly not manage the hospital alone; Doctor Morland's
offer had merely made it easy for all to leave without losing
face. He, Li San-djiu-tz, could not accept it—they had
done too much for him. "Meng Ih-hseng, I also remain," he
said briefly, while his mind made a secret reservation: If
things become too bad, you can join that band in the Hills!

After the meeting Doctor Morland and Hu Ih-hseng were
in the office together for some time. Later, the Chinese physician called San-djiu aside to say, "You and I are advised
to leave. The enemy, it seems, dislikes educated Chinese,
particularly the foreign trained."

"And I?"

"The youngest here and strong! Sent to Japan as a prisoner, you could do much work in their fields."

Li was speechless. Here was something to fear more than anything yet heard. "Have they no workers of their own?" he finally gasped.

"Most of their youths come here to fight. Already too many Chinese boys have been seized and carried over the sea."

"Never will I go there, never! Better to die here!"

"Truly! The day they arrive we will hide—so I promised Meng Ih-hseng. Some of their officers and troops, it is said, are better than others. Perhaps those at Nanking were the worst. What kind comes here——" he shrugged his shoulders in an expressive gesture. "If need be, we can find our way to the hiding place in the Hills. Are you willing, or not?"

"Can do!" the youth answered. If Hu Doctor dared to stay he could do no less, though the recurring thought of being sent to Japan still hung over him like doom.

For two days the Red Cross truck carried patients from rural districts back to their homes. Most of those whose families dwelt close by preferred in the event of trouble to remain beneath the protection of the American flag.

On the third morning the Captain, still thin and pale, climbed into the machine with his men and drove away. Where they were bound no one save those in the company knew. Shortly before departure, the officer sought out Li to say, "Many times have I wished to speak of gratitude to you. But where can a man find words to thank another for so great a gift?"

"It was too little—too little!" Thirty-nine hastened to protest.

The other waved the politeness aside. "Since our country fights a war, we may not again meet. Therefore, let me give you this." He held out an unsealed envelope bearing a name and address. "Within is a letter to my family. I have written another of explanation and sent that by post. In time of need, forward this to them. They are not entirely without influence nor do they forget debts easily."

Embarrassment made the youth tongue-tied. To ease the moment, the Captain finished lightly with a smile, "Li Orderly, History is filled with tales of blood brothers; truly, you and I are half brothers at least." With a parting phrase, "May your fortune be good!" he had gone on his way.

Later, San-djiu examined envelope and enclosed sheet carefully. Unable to read it himself, he would some day ask Hu Ih-hseng to do so. Meanwhile, since there was no way of guessing the contents, it might be wise to wear the letter safely hidden in his belt.

Noon of the same day brought word that the enemy was only ten *li* from Y——. The defenders re-enforced by a few National Government troops had taken strategic positions, it was said; but as the average thinking citizen feared, these forces offered no formidable obstacle to Japan's mechanized army. There seemed no good reason to hope that the invaders could be held off later than nightfall.

In the middle of the afternoon the distinctive sound of a great explosion was added to that of the familiar gun fire.

Later, airplanes that had droned above the community for days disappeared southward, and a surprising lull settled over the countryside.

Sunset flamed and faded. Untouched as usual by affairs below, the sky darkened with studied effect to set off a pale crescent moon of early spring. Gradually, against the silvered yellow light twisting rows of city roof tops were penciled in detail. Beneath them, families huddled together to wait for the worst. Through the afternoon, officials and many other citizens had fled elsewhere. Only those chained by indecision in the face of danger or the inescapable responsibilities of illness, birth, or death, remained behind the boarded house fronts. There, besieged before the city was even attacked, they continued hoping unreasonably that what had happened in the other cities, in Nanking—above all, in Nanking—might not be repeated here.

Tonight ambitious parents gave little thought to children's education or betrothals. Merchants planned no gainful deals for tomorrow or the days to follow. Students did not bother to riffle the pages of the books that lay at hand. Instead, old and young, wise and foolish, clung together in each household group and entertained the uninvited guests whose names were Misery and Fear.

At the hospital, tension increased with each hour. Workers, usually only too glad to be relieved of duty, this evening moved restlessly up and down the dimly lighted corridors in search of something to do. With only twenty patients left time hung heavily on everyone's hands.

In the endeavor to create an atmosphere of normalcy,
the two physicians sat at a chess board in the lower reception hall as they sometimes did in rare moments of leisure.
Tonight they used the tall ivory figures of the Chinese
game. These represented generals and armies instead of
Western bishops, queens, and knights. In the past, Thirty-
nine, waiting on call, had watched such contests with interest, but this one seemed too symbolic of the actual struggle being staged on roads near by. That within a few short
hours, the citizens of Y——, and perhaps all here in the
hospital as well, might be sacrificed like the pawns on the
board was much too probable for comfort.

This was his third such night within six moons, he thought,
turning toward a window and looking out into the moonlight.
The first had been in the cave where Old Head lay helplessly sleeping while the Japanese vessels rode the tides
below and the Lieutenant made the dangerous way back
from the fields. The rushes at Chi Farmer's had hidden
Grandfather and himself on the second occasion, and the
memory of all that had happened then made his body chill.
Very different were the present circumstances. Here, with
companions all around, he stood in a foreign *Ih-yuen* pro-
tected by an American flag, and Lao To was no longer
beside him. For the first time since his grandfather's death,
he felt peculiarly comforted—this affair, at least, Old Head
need not endure.

After a while the physicians ended their game and began
the bedtime rounds. Li, sent off duty, went uneasily to his
room. The night world seemed held in ominous silence.

Even the usual sounds of cook and his cronies arguing in the kitchen below were not to be heard. What were the invaders doing there in the moonlight on the outskirts of the city? Or were they sleeping? The strange thought came to him that resting in camp Japanese soldiers might be simply weary and homesick men.

It was nearly dawn before San-djiu slept and almost at once he was awakened by terrific clamor. Staccato explosions from small arms were punctuated by much greater ones from shells and bombs. Again airplanes whirred above and this time loosed their destructive loads upon the city. No pursuit ships rose in challenge; most of China's air equipment lay in fragments on fields between the Coast and Nanking. The atmosphere was heavy with acrid smoke, and a thin veil of gray hung over the compound.

As Doctor Morland had expected, in the hour of peril many citizens turned to the hospital as their only haven in the midst of desolation. Mothers, disheveled and unkempt, carrying infants in their arms; men bending beneath the burden of aged parents or bundles of household possessions; children screaming in the effort to keep from being trampled underfoot, all pled for entrance to the Healing Hall.

The old gateman, having unbarred the great wooden doors for the first small group, could no more have stemmed the tide of frantic people that pressed after these than he could have dammed the Yangtze in flood. Only when most of the hospital workers rushed to his assistance, were the doors finally closed and barred again.

Attempting to take stock of the situation from the vantage point of the steps, Doctor Morland's mind ached with sympathy for the crowd stranded in the street outside the gate. Yet, with hospital patients the first consideration, he dared not take in too many refugees to handle safely. Fortunately the weather was clear, but after sunset the temperature still fell sharply, and infants and aged would then have to be sheltered in the building. Aside from the possibility of bombing and an ensuing panic, food was his greatest concern. These people in their hurried evacuation from homes had probably salvaged little to eat. At present the hospital had sufficient supplies for those inside, but more might be unobtainable. Always the chief task for Japanese troops of occupation was to seize every available ounce of food.

He watched the mass of people at first drifting aimlessly as autumn leaves about the lawn and garden ways but soon settling to earth in family groups. Like most Chinese in distress, when urgency lessened these showed the characteristics of courtesy and thoughtfulness. Deeply grateful for refuge, they wished to cause no unnecessary trouble. Babies were nursed, the aged made comfortable, and children forced to behave quietly. In a surprisingly short time comparative order ruled.

From somewhere in a group near by came a deep-throated chuckle of amusement, and the physician's eyes lighted at the sound. What a gift this race had for cheerful endurance in suffering, he thought with admiration. Uprooted from their homes and aware that the next moment might bring further terrors, still they could laugh. If the present government under Chiang Kai-shek could unite them, they might become, regardless of poor equipment, an unconquerable obstacle to Japan's ambitions. Issuing a few simple orders to the helpers, he re-entered the building.

Li, removing a two-year-old boy from some shrubs recently set out, overheard a man with the stained fingers of a metal-worker exclaim, "Whether soldiers or someone else—what matter who did the good deed?"

"What good deed is this?" he asked the speaker.

"Have you not heard? Yesterday in the Hour of the Sheep a Japanese train was wrecked outside the city. Hundreds of their soldiers were hurt or killed, it is said. For that reason they did not reach here until this morning."

"When trouble cannot be escaped, what value is one night more or less?" querulously broke in an old man.

"None, Grandfather, but to have many 'dwarfs' perish *is* important."

So the band in the Hills had been busy, Thirty-nine told himself.

In a short time Y—— was completely in enemy hands. Fires still raged but the heavy noises of battle had ceased.

"Li Orderly, Hu Ih-hseng wants you," a servant called out.

The youth found both physicians in the office. "Doctor Morland thinks you and I should go away for a little," Hu Ih-hseng said. "At any time the Japanese may come here."

A repeated hammering at the front entrance now brought the gateman rushing in. "Meng Ih-hseng, Meng Ih-hseng," he interrupted breathlessly, "Japanese wait outside."

"How many?"

"Eight, perhaps ten. Through that crack in the wall I counted." The old man was shaking—he had heard too many tales of bayoneted gatemen.

"Go to the gate, but do not open it until I come!" The speaker turned swiftly to Hu Ih-hseng. "It is too late to hide elsewhere. Get some bandages on your head and Li's and go to bed in the empty ward! Remember to act like patients! Now hurry! While you prepare, I will try to keep them downstairs." The next moment the American was running down the walk after the gateman.

On the floor above, Hu Ih-hseng and Thirty-nine bandaged hastily, tore off clothing, and stuffed this in a hamper. Then slipping on garments customarily supplied to patients, they got into beds. Hu whispered the warning, "Li, lie on your side, close your eyes, and keep your hands under the covers. They do not look like a sick man's."

Footsteps could now be heard approaching, and a minute later Meng Ih-hseng appeared with three Japanese officers in the doorway. Thirty-nine flashed a glance at the group, then lowered eyelids to slits.

One of the officers came forward, counted empty beds, and stared at the patients in turn. In Chinese he called across the room, "When do these leave?"

"Soon," Doctor Morland replied calmly.

The leader of the party, a portly man wearing several medals, asked abruptly, "You have a Chinese doctor on your staff, not so?"

"Yes."

"Send for him."

"At the moment he is off duty."

"In the building?"

"Major, my assistant's free time is his own affair. Usually he leaves a note in English on my desk, giving hours of departure and return. Would you like to read that for yourself?"

The officer's reply was brusque. "Not important."

In another moment they had moved on down the hall. Thirty-nine's heart was pounding. How had Hu Ih-hseng endured this conversation? He looked at the physician but if the other had been having bad moments, his face showed no signs.

Shortly afterwards Doctor Morland returned to the ward alone, closed the door firmly behind him, and sat wearily on the edge of the bed. "It must have been a great strain to lie there and listen, Hu, but I had to work fast," he said in English.

"Too bad you do not play *mah pai*, Doctor, you would be very successful," Hu replied. "How did you know they did not read English?"

"The Honorable Major made one miserable attempt to speak it, no more; so I took a chance on his not being able to read the language." He paused a second, then went on, "You must leave at once and take Li with you."

San-djiu had been lying there understanding nothing, and in courtesy Doctor Morland suddenly changed to Chinese. "In their camp are many wounded. I think the plan is for you to work there."

"So?" the other murmured. "Then they do not bring their wounded here?"

"Would that were true! They counted every empty bed."

"And our patients?"

"Stay until recovered. The refugees in the yard also remain unmolested, although many will now be too frightened to stay."

"How did you win such concessions?"

"By reminding that I was under orders to work in a hospital for Chinese; if this could not be done the place would be closed, and the United States Consular Seal put on the doors." He smiled wryly. "Their leader's next remark was, 'Accidents often happen to deserted foreign property.'

" 'Too bad, is it not?' I asked. 'For instance, the accident to the United States gunboat, *Panay*, has been very expensive for your country, Honorable Major, do you not agree?' His hearing seemed suddenly to be poor."

"But they can seize the hospital and run it themselves, Doctor."

"Certainly. However, these particular troops apparently lack medical attendants; some of the doctors may have been killed in that train wreck. So this *Ih-yuen* is useful."

"What of Meng Si-mu and Beh Hsiao-je?"

The American looked down at his hands for a long moment. "They are determined to stay and work. It is my hope that the Government at Washington will send them home," he said heavily. "Now let us think up a plan for you two. Already the wounded may be coming here."

"Is the front entrance guarded?"

"Yes, but not the small gate in the alley."

Hu threw aside the covers and got out of bed. The other physician's lips broadened into a smile. "Your bandaging is not up to its usual standard, Doctor," he commented, and abruptly laughter eased nervous tension for the three of them.

Within a half hour, two men in laborer's outfits, each carrying a bundle in faded blue cotton cloth, emerged from the rear entrance of the hospital and made their way north into the country. Refugees were still crowding the main road in this section, but the two newcomers cut across a field path to the west and later turned southward.

As the sun was setting, they came to the foot of a hill and there sank down in a thicket to wait for dusk. For a time each seemed lost in his own thoughts, then the younger spoke, "Truly, Honorable Doctor, I did not know a foreigner could be like that!"

His companion studied him through narrowed lids. "Li, Race does not make men good or bad. Meng Ih-hseng, whatever his nation, would be a good man and a fine doctor." He sighed. "Today that is the trouble with the world: each country thinks it is best. In Europe, Germany; in Asia, Japan. For centuries, China was as foolish; at present we suffer for our blindness of the past."

San-djiu looked up inquiringly. "I do not ten-tenths understand."

"For many centuries our Middle Kingdom was rich and strong, loving peace and civilization. We thought all other people barbarians and wished no dealings with them, for their ways were rough and warlike. As time went on, evil emperors came to the Dragon Throne and the nation weakened under their rule. Meanwhile the countries beyond the sea grew stronger, and China was a prize that tempted all. In each generation some of our wise men saw the danger and struggled against it. During the present century there have been many: Sun Yat-sen, Founder of the Republic in 1911; Hu Shih, the scholar who modernized our language and learning; Generalissimo Chiang Kai-shek, the present Leader; and others. But, 'When the boat is in midstream it is too late to mend the leak,' " he quoted. "Today Japan fights with the most modern weapons and many of them; China's are old-fashioned and few." He paused as if overcome by the gravity of the situation.

"So the Lieutenant told me," San-djiu said. "How then can we hope to win?"

Hu Ih-hseng smiled a little sadly. "China always has one hope—her people!" Glancing up at the sky, he added, "Now we can go."

Later, after clambering over the hillside they were ordered to halt.

The doctor gave the usual password, "National Salvation."

"National Salvation," returned the other. "You are a friend?"

"The doctor named Hu."

"And your companion?"

"Li, hospital attendant."

"No others?"

"No others."

Soon the now familiar entrance swung open and they were ushered within. The cave was deserted. "You alone are here?" Hu Ih-hseng asked.

"Yes. Tonight there is much to do. Later the rest will return."

"Have you food?"

Hastily lighting a candle, the man showed them where to find the necessary things, then hurried outside to his duty as guard.

Having eaten, the two in the cave took *pu-gai* from their bundles and arranged them on the floor. Then carefully examining his bag of instruments and drugs, the doctor placed it close at hand.

San-djiu reached inside garments and pulling out a paper, handed it to the physician. "Today, after I threw my clothes in the basket I worried about this, fearing someone might destroy it while we were in the ward. Perhaps, Honorable Doctor, you will tell me whether it is important."

Hu Ih-hseng studied the envelope and letter. Slowly he began to translate.

At the end, Thirty-nine protested, "You and Meng Ih-hseng did much more for the Captain."

"Lay down your heart—the officer did not forget the hospital." Continuing he said, "Wear it on your body. Who can say when such a letter may be of great use?"

"And the writing on the envelope?"

"I forgot to tell you that. It is addressed to someone named Yen, at the official residence in Kunming."

"Where is that?"

"In Yunnan, a far western province."

Li thanked him and put the letter safely away. The Captain had written his people that he owed life to Li, an orderly in the hospital at Y——, and wished them to remember. Truly, those were kind words. However, the orderly named Li was not likely to use the message, for he had no desire to deal with people in official residences, whether in that strange province or here close by.

With *pu-gai* rolled about him, the youth lay in the dim cavern and thought of the past six moons. Events stood out almost as clearly as if painted on scrolls. In that short space of time much sorrow had come, for Lao To and their home had both been lost. Fisherman, farmer, orderly, thus had he advanced in work. While doing so the gods had given him strange and unusual friends. Tonight where were the Lieutenant and the Captain, alive or dead? Had Hsiao Pan received his letter? How was Doctor Morland managing a hospital crowded with Japanese? Such were the questions running through his mind, and flowing like a dark current beneath these were the much graver ones about China itself.

One hope there was, Hu Ih-hseng had said, one hope— the people. Who were the people? The hardworking farmers and artisans; those dry-eyed refugees whose tears flowed into their stomachs; the little girls in the camp trying to remember what an absent mother had taught; these Righteous Fighters who worked by day and fought at night; and the ill-equipped officers and soldiers! Hu Doctor himself was one; and he, Li San-djiu-tz, another. An unfamiliar sense of brotherhood warmed his heart. "China's hope, her people," the words repeated themselves. Drowsing, he saw a vast company of figures stepping from forty centuries of history into the shadowy cave. "China's people," they whispered in promise, "China's people—they shall save the land, they shall save the land!"

Part III. THE FREE LAND

CHAPTER XI

"Dragons Beget Dragons"

FOR more than five months Hu Ih-hseng and Li lived with the Righteous Fighters in the Hills. The arrival of a physician and an assistant to care for the wounded seemed a special favor of Fortune to all in the band. Now that Y—— and its lines of communications were under enemy control, guerrilla operations were becoming much more difficult than before, and casualties increased proportionately.

The personnel of the group changed overnight. Most of the original members had been citizens of Y——. These, forewarned on the fateful morning of invasion, had hurried back to the city to shoulder family responsibilities, and a few only had effected a return to the hideout.

Vacancies left by absentees were immediately filled, though, from the surrounding countryside, and before long the company was several times its former size. The homeless among them erected carefully camouflaged shelters of boughs and leaves on the hillside, for the cave was too small to hold so many and was used chiefly as hospital and council chamber.

By what means the latest guerrillas had learned of the "underground" organization, San-djiu never knew. Most were from scattered villages and farms with few outside contacts. Aggression, however, never failed to stir to fresh flame the banked fires of Freedom in men's hearts. By every passing wind the smoking signals were picked up and carried to the conquered; in this way, doubtless, the word of secret resistance had reached the present victims of oppression.

If the old and new members differed in backgrounds, their personal experiences varied still more. The first had been farsighted patriots who, not having met the foe, prepared against his advance; these others were fragments of human wreckage left behind in the trail of Japanese conquest. They had lost homes and means of livelihood. Some had been forced to stand by helplessly while children and aged parents were killed. As many more had themselves been machine-gunned from the air or bayoneted and left for dead. Being alive and for the moment out of enemy reach seemed a miracle. Wounded and uninjured alike had a single purpose left in life—to strike back at the source of all their suffering.

With deep interest Thirty-nine watched these grim, embittered farmers as they came and went on the dangerous missions assigned them. Tillers of the soil were proverbially unconcerned about national affairs; they were also slow to anger. In all the farm land between the Point and Y—— the youth had found no one disturbed over events except Hsiao Pan. Yet Hu Ih-hseng had told him that most of the revolts in China's long history had been fomented by such men. Certainly the present ones in the camp counted no risk too great if it might bring results. Even the wounded among them begrudged every hour needed for recovery.

"That countrymen should be so hot-hearted is hard to believe," Li said one morning helping Hu Ih-hseng to roll bandages from strips of cotton rags.

"My grandmother had a saying, 'They have broken up the cooking pots and sunk the boats,' " replied the physician. "Desperate men recognize no obstacles."

This attitude was not limited to the district around Y——; the determination to resist was stiffening all over China. Throughout the occupied territory mushroom growths of rebellion sprang up overnight in the most unlikely locations. Temples, thatched farm huts, teahouses, and shops become secret meeting places. Many of these were in devastated towns and cities where enemy soldiers patrolled thoroughfares a few feet away.

The Chinese Army, retreating inland after the first terrific defeats, was now getting its second wind and holding back the invaders on several fronts. When Nanking fell, the victorious Japanese had boasted that Hankow, the temporary capital of the Central Government, would also fall within a few weeks. They were still a long way from achieving this when Taierchuang to the north demanded their attention. In that city the Generalissimo's troops aided by guerrillas won a tremendous victory against a huge Nipponese force, and for the first time the Chinese people felt hopeful about the outcome of the nation-wide struggle. Rejoicing found expression in celebration everywhere, and fresh waves of "underground" activities surged on the tides of feeling.

Drunk with power from an almost unbroken sequence of victories, the Japanese now unexpectedly found themselves in the position of men armed to fight tigers and attacked by swarms of angry bees. The complete defeat at Taierchuang had set them back on their heels; the growth of civilian warfare seemed about to become even more disastrous. Much of the work their engineers accomplished by daylight the Righteous Fighters rendered useless during the night. Rails were ripped up; munition dumps fired; bridges and important roadways mined. Lone sentinels guarding strategic points disappeared as strangely as if the earth had opened to swallow them. The few who lived to report such assaults were unable when questioned to give much information.

"At the time of the incident you saw no Chinese?"

"None, Sir. Earlier at dusk a beggar sat beside the road, but I hurried him on his way."

"You had no warning of approach?"

"Once in the night, Sir, a bird called. There was no other sound."

"At night few birds call. What kind was this?"

"Sir, I come from a cotton mill in Yokohama; I know little about birds."

"What do you know?" thundered the examining officer.

"About two hours before dawn, Sir, hands closed about my throat. But for a trick learned in jiujitsu, I should not be here."

"And the assailant?"

"Though badly wounded, Sir, he escaped."

The other reports were much like this in character; in each instance the element of surprise had been the most important factor. Guards were doubled, then trebled; but they went to their posts in terror nonetheless, for attacks continued with unabated success.

Expecting little opposition from the conquered, Nipponese Headquarters had not counted on extensive policing of rural sections. This new development necessitated taking men from other duties, and the lines of invasion were already stretched so long and thin that subtractions could be ill-afforded. In reprisal whole villages were wiped out, but the punishment served merely as added impetus to offenders.

The Japanese felt certain that many of the farmers remaining on the land were involved in the sabotage and killing, but who they were was the problem to be solved. Searching of homes and questioning under torture revealed no information from the countrymen. Moreover, the invaders, using confiscated supplies much faster than replacements could be made, were dependent on the farm people for new crops. Yet even those Chinese who appeared most co-operative had startlingly poor harvests.

To conquer territory was one thing; to make the conquest pay was something else. Japan's eventual plan was to rule all Asia; to succeed she must first force China to supply raw materials and foodstuffs—otherwise the fruits of victory in this land would be worthless. Since severity did not make the Chinese submissive, a program of assumed friendliness might accomplish better results; and the idea should be tested at once.

Y—— presented an excellent example of occupied territory subjected to both methods. From the day of invasion it had been a city without a soul. Strangely enough the destruction caused by bombs and fires had little to do with this change in spirit, for streets had already been cleared of debris. Instead, the pale ghost of the formerly thriving community stalked in districts that bore no marks of battle.

Many buildings were empty; those still occupied showed little evidence of life inside. The women and children who had dared to remain in the city hid in darkened rooms. Men ventured out of doors only when their errands could no longer be delayed. Gay advertising banners fluttered uselessly above stores that had neither stocks nor customers. Gone were the sounds of busy trade, the good-natured badinage of Chinese street crowds, the enticing odors from food shops and venders' trays. Only the martial click of booted heels and the harsh commands issued to slave labor could be heard on thoroughfares that had once echoed to the clamor of normal living.

Under the new program merchants and artisans were encouraged to resume business. When frightened citizens now came on the streets, their conquerors greeted them with wide, toothy smiles instead of insults. Posters appeared everywhere on empty wall space. One read: "Japan is China's best friend. China must free herself of evil leaders like Chiang Kai-shek; then her troubles will end." Another bore the picture of a Japanese soldier giving sweets to a Chinese youngster. It was very popular with the Army of Occupation.

In the guerrilla camp the changed tactics were watched with grim amusement; and in a game of cat and mouse, the saboteurs lessened activities for a time. The stirring to life of the dead community, relaxed patrols, freer communications between farms and markets, all furthered the patriots' own plans for the future. During the lull the men in the hill cave spent most of their time carefully mapping out campaigns. Occasionally some member, disguised as a farmer carrying vegetables, risked life to slip into Y—— and study the opportunities offered by the present situation. Sometimes these scouts carried back to their comrades poster-samples of Japanese propaganda. The fact that they had been removed from under the enemy's very eyes supplied entertainment for the camp and at the same time deeply annoyed the Japanese.

When conditions were exactly as the Righteous Fighters wished, operations were renewed on a major scale. Hu Ih-hseng and San-djiu now frequently accompanied the active participants within a *li* or so of enemy lines. There in some farm shed they would wait for the others to return. Giving First Aid close to the scene of action helped to save men too severely wounded to stand the longer journey to the cave.

When urgency forced physician and helper into occupied territory, they sought refuge usually in poorly patrolled hamlets. One of these was known as The Village of Wu Widow's Arch. This memorial to a widow famed for virtue and benevolence had been built several centuries earlier. Since that time the community clustered about it had experienced the usual vicissitudes of war, drought, flood, and famine. The stone arch, however, had managed in some way to escape all harm save that wrought by Time and Weather; and inhabitants still pointed to it proudly as the outstanding piece of architectural beauty in the vicinity.

Set in grain fields, the village acted as a center of exchange between the farms and Y———. There were about eighty or ninety one-storied buildings, including an inn and perhaps ten shops. These faced each other across the highway which the National Government had constructed a year earlier.

When Japanese troops marched through, the village experienced what had now become an old story in occupied territory. Livestock, food supplies, and all other articles that the invaders considered useful or desirable were seized. At least half the population had fled in advance; of those who remained, some were killed and more wounded. In this instance, though, buildings were not destroyed, and within a few days the unhappy people began picking up the torn threads of life and weaving them into a new pattern.

The conquering army left behind three representatives, a corporal and two subordinates, to keep order in the community and the adjacent countryside. The corporal was a lonely young man, who had been taken from his regular work

of teaching a primary school in Osaka in order to serve with
the forces in China. Back in Japan his eighteen-year-old
wife was having great difficulty eking out a living for herself
and their infant son. The husband, constantly worried about
his family and longing for the more peaceful pursuits of the
classroom, had little heart for enforcing discipline on The
Village of Wu Widow's Arch. He was not the type to see
subversive activities where none existed, and his days offered
no greater distraction than that of sitting in the deserted
house chosen as headquarters and receiving reports from the
two assistants.

Diagonally opposite his quarters was the establishment of
Chen, the grain merchant. This, the largest shop in the neighborhood, had a more elaborate grill work at the entrance
than even the teahouse. Behind the store were two comfortable living rooms. These contained some good pieces of
redwood furniture, a pair of antique wall scrolls, attractive
porcelain flower jars, and a small cupboard of books. The
room at the rear boasted the foreign innovation of glass win-
dow-lights instead of the usual oiled paper. Here was the
merchant's favorite spot in his home; from it one looked out
on the village pool a few yards distant.

During the greater part of the year, the pool was alive
with action from dawn to dusk. There the women knelt to
wash garments by beating them on stones. Little maids
rinsed baskets of green vegetables in preparation for the
day's main meal. Boys too young for other tasks led
shui-niu into the water to bathe; and infants, tied by a strip
of cotton cloth to guardians, dug happily for treasure in the

mud. All of these affairs were carried on to the cheerful ac-
companiment of quacking ducks, barking dogs, and an
unceasing flow of gossipy chatter.

In the winter months the pool was a much quieter place,
but it was then that Chen most enjoyed the sunsets. At such
hours the darkened water was ruffled by chill winds, and the
shivering willows holding magpie nests aloft seemed to be
offering obeisance to a cold, yellow sky.

At present the grain merchant spent most of the time in
the shop with a book. Two sons, students in Nanking before
the War, had left school to join the Army, and so far definite
word of only one had been received. The youngest boy,
aged eleven, had been sent with his mother and sister to a
place of safety before the enemy's arrival. An elderly village housewife came in to prepare food, but aside from that
Chen had surprisingly few contacts with others.

Previous to the trouble, the grain merchant, possessing a
reputation for integrity and a little learning as well, had been
one of the most popular and respected men in the community.
Now, however, to neighbors' horrified astonishment, Chen
showed every sign of co-operating with the enemy. From
the beginning he had been friendly to the corporal. At
almost any hour the Japanese, who like all the teachers in
his home district had been forced to learn Chinese and spoke
the language fairly well, might be seen in the grain shop.
Sometimes the two men discussed bits from an open book
lying on the counter. On other occasions they sat and sipped
tea, talking amiably as old acquaintances might do. Once
Chen had actually taken this questionable guest to the rear

room for a view of the sunset. Several people had seen them
standing there together watching the magpies fly down from
their nests in the willows and move woodenly about the pool
edge in search of food.

The spectators had been shocked beyond description by the
latest display of intimacy, and from that moment doubts in
villagers' minds changed to certainties. Business was slowly
recovering from the invasion, but this was not true in Chen's
case. Farmers who had formerly come first to him, now
took their products elsewhere. The housewife suddenly
found her duties at home too urgent to prepare his food,
and old friends avoided the grain shop with careful cal-
culation.

San-djiu, having heard a number of references in the cave
to the friendship between Chen and the Japanese, wondered
why the band had selected the empty house next the grain
merchant's for a First Aid Station. Certainly it was dangerous enough to be in an occupied village; to hide next door
to a traitor seemed to him an unnecessary risk. On the first
two visits, though, everything went smoothly enough; on the
third, trouble occurred.

Dusk had not yet deepened to night when Hu Ih-hseng, a
guerrilla sentry, and Li slipped through the fields, passed the
pool, and made their way to the empty building. Having
seen them safely there, the sentry disappeared in the swiftly
thickening shadows.

Within the house Thirty-nine, sensing afresh the insecurity
of this refuge, asked the physician abruptly, "The grain merchant next door, is he too stupid to notice us?"

Hu Ih-hseng hesitated for a second then said, "Come! Tonight we shall wait in the front room." Together they tiptoed there through the darkness. The doctor moved softly, his ear pressed close to the wall adjacent to the grain shop. After a moment or two he whispered, "Here is the place." Quietly the two sat down to listen beside a specially prepared panel that offered little barrier to sound.

For a time there was silence, but it was broken soon by the approach of someone in military boots. After a polite exchange of greetings, the merchant and the corporal talked of many things: the weather; the condition of crops; the poet T'ao Yuan-ming of the Fourth Century, whose enthusiasm for the chrysanthemum had made it a favorite national flower. Listening, Li thought to himself that, while interesting, such talk could hardly be useful to the band. Yet in this very house, scouts had learned several items of great importance. One had led to the wrecking of a train that carried a Japanese general and his aides to their death.

After an hour or so, the corporal bade his host good night, and soon the merchant could be heard sliding the wooden panels into their grooves at the entrance. The work of closing the shop must have been nearly completed when some-one else pushed inside.

Next door the listeners heard Chen say quietly, "Lin, a long time has passed since you were under my roof. Any affair that brings you here so late must be important."

"You have spoken truly. The business concerns two lives —yours and mine." The speaker was breathing shortly with emotion. "When the Eastern-Ocean 'devils' came here, they

killed my only son and his mother. This you knew, but perhaps you have forgotten."

"No, I have not forgotten. I grieve for your loss."

Lin's voice was rough with contempt. "Of a certainty
your grief has a strange pattern, for you, an old friend, kow-
towed to the murderers. When the two in my house died, my
heart died also. I cannot work. Food is tasteless and sleep
comes rarely. Tonight I resolved to eat poison; but first,
I said, my good knife shall rid China of one traitor. When
that deed is done, I shall go more easily to my own grave."
He paused to end dramatically, "You are that man!"

There was a sharp scuffle in the room, then for a second
the merchant seemed to have placed some barrier between
himself and his assailant. His voice, still low, had deepened
with urgency. "Lin, listen a little! You say I forget your
son's death. Do you wish to know what they did to *my*
first-born at Nanking?" The words were now pouring from
Chen's lips in a flood. "He and fifty of his company were
made to dig a pit. When it was large enough, the Japanese
threw foreign oil down on the diggers, set them afire, and
buried them in the pit. My son's friend, a comrade who had
escaped, sent me word."

"Then—then you. . . . ?" Lin gasped.

"No, I have not betrayed China, though you and others
like you who have known me all my life could believe that
without difficulty," finished the merchant bitterly.

"But the Japanese. . . . . ?" came the further protest.

"The 'dwarf' in charge here is a young man and careless
in speech. Some of the things he has said have been useful

to our cause." Chen sighed deeply, then added, "Go home and tell no one what you have learned. Also, do not again talk foolishly of eating poison; only weak men use such methods. If you wish to help your country, in the future I can tell you a way. At present continue to avoid me; our neighbors must not yet see any change in our relationship." Chen's speech ended abruptly.

The Japanese corporal must have reappeared without warning, for the listeners next door were horrified to hear his voice now interrupt sharply, "Honorable Merchant, there will be no further need to avoid you——you will not be here."

Hu Ih-hseng was already on his feet. "Hurry!" he whispered to Li. Together they hastened stealthily through the house. Outside, the doctor imitated a magpie's cawing, and at once the guerrilla sentry answered the call.

Without waiting for the physician, San-djiu rushed through the rear entrance of Chen's house and into the store. In the middle of the room stood the Japanese with his revolver covering the two men. As Thirty-nine entered, the other fired at the grain merchant, then swerved toward the newcomer. Catching up a heavy stool, Li swung it. It crashed on the corporal's head, but not before the gun spat fire for a second time. At the same moment Lin jumped with his knife.

In the street one of the Nipponese patrols returning to report to his superior was startled by the sound of shots and started on the run in that direction. He squeezed through the front entrance a second after Hu Ih-hseng and the sentry came in at the back, but that second cost him his life.

Catching up a heavy stool, Li swung it.

As the fracas quieted, the doctor attended to Chen's wound which, though deep, was not in a vital spot. Whether the former schoolmaster's marksmanship was poor or whether the surprise of Li's entrance had affected his aim, no one would ever know.

"More four-inch bandage!" called the physician, and San-djiu, reaching for the article, felt his arm go suddenly limp. He looked down. His jacket sleeve was stained with blood.

"Here—lie on the floor!" Hu Ih-hseng commanded, and the youth who was beginning to sway with dizziness promptly obeyed.

In the meanwhile the inhabitants, roused from sleep by the noise, crowded into the store. On the floor lay two dead Japanese, the wounded Chen, and a strange youth. The villagers stared at the doctor, who was much too busy to pay any attention to them.

Lin, recognizing that he himself had been the direct cause of the present trouble, put aside personal unhappiness and stepped forward. Considering the moment for secrecy past, he gave a brief account of the affair and asked for volunteers to help capture the other patrol. It was highly important that no alarm reach the next Japanese outpost until the village had time to settle on a course of action.

Within a few minutes the searching party led by the sentry and Lin started up the road, and the remaining inhabitants returned home to pack for evacuation. No alternative was left to them; not one was so foolish as to think he could continue in this doomed community and live.

An hour later the searchers, having satisfactorily accounted
for their quarry, returned; and shortly afterwards the guerrillas came in from the night's work bearing two injured companions. Between midnight and daybreak all country paths
connecting the village with unoccupied territory were crowded.

When the Japanese Headquarters received no early morning report from this section, they sent troops to investigate
the silence. Several families of magpies and a mangy dog
or two were the only living creatures to be found. In a few
hours even these were gone. What had once been a prosperous little community had become a charred and level strip,
and the stone Memorial Arch to the virtuous Widow named
Wu stood black and stark beneath a pitiless sun.

Later in the hill cave, San-djiu, trying to forget the throb-
bing in his arm, found thought confused by the happenings
of the night. So Chen had not been a traitor, and the magpie
cawing heard on every visit had not been bird calls but signals between the grain merchant and the guerrillas. He
could still see the corporal slumping to the floor and hear the
wounded Chen murmuring, "Poor youth! He belonged in
a schoolroom, not here in this uniform."

The grain merchant, who with Lin had accompanied the
guerrillas back to camp, was a strange man. Moved by patriotism and personal grief, Chen had risked both reputation
and life to strike at the enemy. But even while he drew military secrets from the young Japanese he had pitied him.

War changed men. From infancy Thirty-nine had been
taught that violence of any sort was wrong. Yet tonight he
himself had struck a blow that made a man easy prey for

another's knife thrust. "Dragons beget dragons," Lao To had often said, "and evil men make others evil, also."

Only a short time ago these Righteous Fighters in the cave had been peace-loving citizens. Now there was nothing, however horrible, they would not do, provided it harmed the invaders. As the conflict continued, were all his people to be driven to such acts? Uneasily he turned, and for a moment everything else was forgotten in the sudden pain of movement.

CHAPTER XII

"It Is Harder to Enter Szechuen Than Heaven"

FOR several days inflammation and pain from the bullet wound kept Li a patient in the cave. On the fourth morning the youth awoke clearheaded and hungry. As he lay still, trying to think through what had happened, Hu Ih-hseng said in greeting, "So you are better!"

"Honorable Doctor, how long have I been here?"

The reply came as a shock. For three days he had not only been useless but had added to the physician's duties as well. After a moment he asked, "When I have eaten, what do you wish me to do?"

"Lie there and gain strength!"

"But, Honorable Doctor, already I am well—look!" Thirty-nine pulled himself up to a sitting posture and immediately fell back. For the next minute or two the world spun about him.

Then Hu Ih-hseng said dryly, "Yes, I see. Now lay down your heart, eat everything you get, and sleep. In two or three days you will be all right." And that, the doctor told himself walking away, was another favor of Fortune, as was every wound recovery treated here where there was no anti-tetanus serum to be administered and very little else in the way of drugs.

For lack of proper medication the grain merchant was in a critical condition. International organizations concerned with medical aid for stricken areas were not yet very active in this particular conflict, which the Japanese for propaganda purposes insisted on calling the China Incident, instead of War. Perhaps some day, Hu's thoughts ran on, the rest of the world would understand more clearly what was really happening. There were still foreign business men who argued that Japan's invasion of China was good for all concerned. He smiled ironically at the idea. Having closed the Lower Yangtze to all commerce but their own, the aggressors were now making roseate promises about reopening this main artery of China trade. If the British, Americans, and French believed such statements, they were stupidly credulous indeed! And when the truth was finally revealed, their opinions about the present invasion would suffer a violent change.

Hu was worried about many things these days. To check the enemy's advance, would the Government break the dykes along the Hwang Ho (Yellow River) as had been threatened, he wondered. How long could Chiang Kai-shek keep the Japanese from taking Hankow? What was actually occurring at the hospital and to the Americans in it? There were few men for whom he cared so much as for Morland and the loss of the other's companionship troubled him sometimes like an aching tooth.

Guerrilla scouts brought back various rumors about the *Ih-yuen*: the foreign women were being sent to America; the doctor would soon close the hospital and follow. Hu thought the first statement probably true; the second he doubted. In two packages of letters forwarded to the camp, Morland had enclosed notes mentioning the difficulties of working under the new regime but saying nothing of leaving. Three weeks had passed, though, since the last arrived, and in that time many things could have happened. There ought to be more soon, Hu told himself, yet the fact that any arrived was amazing.

In occupied areas Japanese censorship had almost completely cut off direct lines of communication with the rest of the world, and the regular postal service had to resort to indirect routes. Foreign mail, for instance, was being flown from Hongkong to Free China where it joined the general post, much of which found its way surprisingly into the right hands, even in territory controlled by the enemy. Throughout Chinese history postal runners had been noted for two things: courage, and faithful attention to business. The war was not changing these characteristics. Life was more difficult for the carriers and demanded greater daring than in peaceful years, but they were accustomed to accepting calamities as a part of professional routine and complained very little. Outwitting the Nipponese, however, afforded some of them great satisfaction, and one example of this was the continued uncensored delivery at the hospital.

Packets of letters were placed in Doctor Morland's hands by the most unexpected people: an incoming patient, a countryman selling vegetables, once even a slop carrier. Where these people had gotten them remained a mystery, for no questions were asked. Meng Ih-hseng had grateful patients all through the district, and it seemed likely that friendly postmen were intercepting communications before they fell into the invader's hands at Y——. Each time in Hu's case, a scout exploring the city had managed to make contact with the Healing Hall and been given the letters.

The day after San-djiu returned to duty, the third lot came to the cave, and to his surprised delight included one for him. Turning it over and over, the youth waited until Hu Ih-hseng was at leisure, then requested a translation. As expected, the sender proved to be Hsiao Pan, although the envelope, the doctor explained, was postmarked in a town some distance from Chi Farm. The crudely written contents were not long. Hsiao Pan inquired solicitously about San-djiu and Old Head; stated in guarded terms that those at present under the Chi roof were well, and the business in which his friend had been interested was prospering. Expressing the hope that Li would write again, he closed with protestations of abiding friendship.

For a moment Thirty-nine sat silent—Hsiao Pan did not yet know Lao To had gone to the ancestors. By way of explanation he said, "That business he speaks of means the guerrillas there are doing good work."

Hu Ih-hseng nodded, but his thoughts had already switched to the questions raised by personal mail. The following morning he called Li aside to say, "Yesterday in a letter the Government asked me to do medical work in Szechuen. I have decided to accept."

"Szechuen is far west, not so?"

"Right."

"But, Honorable Doctor, the war is here."

"When Hankow falls, the Government moves to Chungking. That is the chief port in Szechuen."

Thirty-nine's eyes widened in alarm. "Then they expect Hankow to fall?"

"Each moon the Japanese go farther up the Yangtze, and more of their troops come overland from the north. When the two armies join each other. . . !" With an expressive gesture, he left the sentence unfinished.

"There is no way to stop them?"

"The Generalissimo has decided to break the dykes along the Hwang Ho."

"Break the dykes!" exclaimed the youth, astonished. "What of the people who live near the river?"

"They will eat bitterness, but if this plan helps to save China—*muh iu fa tz*. The Government is warning everybody and is offering each family a little money to pay for moving elsewhere. Also, the western provinces are being asked to find space where the homeless ones may settle."

To destroy the dykes along the Yellow River seemed to Thirty-nine, at first, even worse than Japanese oppression. How many people on the North China Plain would be willing to move before trouble arrived? They were used to floods. Everyone knew that "China's Sorrow" had always changed its course at will. Men fled when the Yellow began to roar and returned as soon as its waters went down. But with the dykes gone, there would be no way left to check the river! Chi Farm would be under water and so would all the country around Y———. Suddenly he said, "It is because of the flood, Honorable Doctor, you go to other work—not so?"

"Six-tenths true! For a time these Righteous Fighters will disband or go elsewhere to fight. But there is a more important reason. Li, the war may last for many years. Chiang Kai-shek shows a great wisdom by moving the Government west. Safe beyond the Yangtze Gorges, our forces may hold off the invaders a long time. Furthermore, some of those western provinces have few people; the land is good and the mountains are rich with metals. There China can begin a new life."

Listening intently, Thirty-nine made no comment and Hu continued, "Meng Ih-hseng also sent me a note. What the scouts said is true—Meng Si-mu and Beh Hsiao-je have both gone to America."

"And the doctor?"

"At the hospital the Japanese have caused too much trouble for him to remain. Instead he goes with a Medical Mission to Yunnan. There the Generalissimo has ordered a ten-thousand-*li* road built over the mountains to Burma, a country south of China."

"Why?"

"So that we may still trade with foreign nations even though the Japanese hold our coast."

"I am very stupid—what will doctors do on that road?"

"The climate is hot and wet, and thousands of people die from the shaking disease (malaria). The Government wishes to find out how to overcome this plague."

San-djiu's ears seemed about to burst. Hankow was expected to fall, the Yellow's dykes were to be broken, Chungking would be the next capital, Hu Ih-hseng would go there, and Meng Ih-hseng to that other place, Yunnan. For a moment the youth felt as if he alone were chained to one spot while all the world moved onward. If his mind had held the hope of returning some day to the Point, Hu Ih-hseng's statement about a long war had ended that. What then could he do? To help build a new China in the west seemed the most exciting of adventures; but such work was for educated men like the physician and not for fishermen and farmers.

As if reading the other's disturbed thoughts, Hu now asked, "Would you like to go with me to Szechuen?"

"Naturally, Honorable Doctor! Does not the chicken long to be a phoenix? What use, though, would I be in important affairs?"

"Do not fear! There will be many more small affairs than great ones. If you wish to go I think it can be arranged."

Li drew a deep breath. "When do we leave, Honorable Doctor?"

"Not too fast!" the physician said with a smile. "First we must travel to Hankow. Since Meng Ih-hseng uses the same route, today I am sending a note asking him to meet us there."

Within three weeks they had reached their first destination, and met Doctor Morland as planned. San-djiu was completely overcome by the strange sights in Hankow, which with Hanyang and Wuchang across the river was China's greatest industrial center as well as the present national capital. The broad Bund on the waterfront was jammed with traffic. All transshipments for Upper River travel had to be made here. Business in Hankow was always heavy; with the Government in residence and countless fleeing-trouble-people passing through, the city was indescribably congested.

Although both physicians were connected with official commissions, they were unable to get three passages on a river steamer for another half month. This boat, going only midway to Chungking, would land them at Ichang. There they would have to find further accommodations on some vessel specially constructed to negotiate Upper Yangtze rapids and whirlpools.

Ichang, when they arrived there, proved to be worse than Hankow. It was difficult to see the river for junks, houseboats, and steamers. To travel by small craft required many weeks; steamers took but a few days. Since most people wanted to reach Chungking in a hurry, the shipping offices were like bedlam. Long lines of applicants waited endless hours for their turns with clerks.

After wasting several days in such fashion, the doctors were able to obtain two passages only on a slow, antiquated steamer.

This, which normally carried one hundred passengers, would now take five hundred sixty. Under existing conditions tickets allowed for nothing but standing room, and all purchasers traveled at their own risk. The fact that so many other people waited to seize these questionable privileges left no hope of better accommodations in the near future, and the two physicians dubiously paid the fares and accepted the terms.

Under the most favorable conditions this slow boat would require seven days for the trip. In case of accident, a common occurrence in the treacherous Gorges, more time might be needed, and the prospect of standing throughout such a trip was far from pleasant. Also, one in the party was still not taken care of; and since Li alone was on no hurried schedule, he would have to be provided for in some other way.

As the two physicians made their exit from the crowded office to the still more crowded street where San-djiu waited, six or seven young men carrying an injured companion opened a path into the nearest teahouse.

"Let's see what is going on," Morland suggested to Hu and followed the others inside.

"If only we knew where to find a doctor!" One of the youths exclaimed aloud as he pushed tortoise shell spectacles back on his nose. "In this place one might as easily discover a unicorn." Glancing up suddenly, the speaker noticed amusement on the face of a tall foreigner near by and said slowly, "Truly, Sir, *you* are not a physician, are you?"

"Not one, two!" Doctor Morland answered, "for my companion here is another. Surely unicorns are nowhere so numerous as that."

The group laughed at this sally, and the spectacled one overwhelmed by the immediate response to a wish could only gasp, "Our fortune is too great!"

Hasty introductions were now exchanged and an explanation given. The young men were from a group of two hundred students who were moving their North China College somewhere between Chungking and Chengtu, Szechuen. Each one carried a small bundle of personal belongings and a much heavier load of college equipment. Those responsible for the library and laboratory equipment pulled their loads in rickshaws. Chu, the injured, whose cart was full of Bunsen burners, had slipped on a loose stone and hurt his right leg.

Within the next few minutes the trouble was professionally diagnosed as a dislocated kneecap, and Chu told that he would do no more walking for some time. Li went hurriedly after Doctor Morland's bag; the proprietor of the establishment provided bamboo for splints; and while the patient lay on a table in the teahouse kitchen, the injury was treated.

Meanwhile the other students were holding a heated discussion about what to do. There seemed nothing left for their disabled companion but to stay here while his schoolmates went on. Already delays on the journey had been numerous, and Chungking by foot travel overland was still several months distant. Furthermore, none possessed funds sufficient to pay for a prolonged halt in Ichang.

Chu, white-faced with pain, waited silently for those about him to reach a decision. "Who will pull the load in my rickshaw?" he finally managed to ask.

Listening, Li realized that the other youth's problem was much greater than his own. Slowly he turned to Hu Ih-hseng and asked in a low voice, *"Hao puh hao,* I take that fellow's cart?"

"All the way to Chungking?"

The physician looked so surprised that Li grinned. "You think, Honorable Doctor, I am not as strong as a student? Since there is no room on the boat, why not go this way?"

Doctor Morland, overhearing the hushed conversation to his left, broke in, "It would be a good deed, Li, and you would have companionship on the way."

San-djiu nodded. "Please, Meng Ih-hseng, ask them what they wish."

On students and patient the effect of the unexpected offer of help was startling. For a few minutes everyone directed compliments toward the completely embarrassed Thirty-nine. The spectacled youth, named Chao Ho-hsan, announced, "We are most unworthy of such great kindness, Li, but if you will pull Chu, we shall be grateful to all future generations in your family. And Chu's load we can divide between us!"

"Though I have never pulled a rickshaw," Thirty-nine replied, "perhaps I can take him and the other things also."

"Truly not, this affair is settled!" the students protested in chorus. "Must a stranger be the only generous one among us?"

With a flourish the irrepressible Chao added in English, "You are too good a sport!"

Both physicians laughed at San-djiu's puzzled expression, and Hu explained, "A good sport means *ting hao tih ren,* Li."

Within an hour San-djiu had made his farewells and started with the students on the long journey to Chungking.

At parting Hu Ih-hseng gave him a small medical kit. "You know how to use all these drugs and dressings, Li," he said. "Keep them for important moments—the sick along the road will be numerous as sea sands. Also, here is the address of the Red Cross in Chungking. Doubtless we shall arrive there long before you, so I shall leave a message with them concerning your future."

Doctor Morland handed the youth some money, and when Thirty-nine protested, said, "Put it in your belt, Li! There was a little due in wages from the hospital and it will buy your food along the way." Flecking at imaginary dust on his sleeve, the American continued, "Helping that student is helping Free China. If you and I do not meet again, remember this—I believe your Old One would be proud." He looked again into the youth's eyes and finished, "Now hurry! those students must not be longer delayed."

On the congested highway San-djiu, learning to manage a rickshaw with the least strain to himself and the greatest comfort to the crippled passenger, hugged in his mind the memory of the recent parting. If pulling Chu helped Free China, then he was already engaged in one of the small affairs of which Hu Ih-hseng had spoken. In such a cause, no difficulty on the road could be too great.

Many times in the long weeks that followed, Thirty-nine had to remind himself of this early enthusiasm. Hampered by the hordes of plodding refugees, the students progressed at a snail's pace. Every step and each turn of the rickshaw wheels had to be watched to keep from injuring children, the sick, and the aged in the endless procession. Most of the older women struggled painfully along on bound feet; grandparents rode pickaback on stalwart sons; frightened, whimpering children clung like limpets to parents' garments in order to avoid separation.

Those who could afford conveyances traveled in rickshaws and sedan chairs, on donkeys and wheelbarrows. Weaving in and out among the others, thousands of coolies dragged heavy loads of machinery, China's salvaged industrial equipment from invaded areas.

Rubbing shoulders with a bearer, Thirty-nine asked curiously, "What do you carry?"

"A cotton gin from Shanghai."

"Where?"

"First to Chungking."

"After that?"

"Only the Government knows."

As the days passed, Li no longer asked about destination, for the answer was always the same—"First to Chungking." Factories for war munitions; silk-filatures; libraries; publishing houses; universities and colleges—all moved across China to Chungking. And with these went China's people— the young and strong, the old and weak, the wealthy, the destitute. Among them were conservative scholars, radical students, ruined merchants, jobless artisans. Homeless exiles, millions in number, they traveled over tortuous highways through strange and inhospitable provinces to reach Chungking and start a new life. At least a third of the number never arrived at the journey's end; but until Death ordered them to halt, they pushed on, hopeful and uncomplaining, toward a future that promised better things.

San-djiu's admiration for his student comrades increased daily. Until the invasion, most of them had never been called upon to endure hardship. Since then many had lost families, friends, and material possessions. Yet on the march, weary and footsore, these youths, with Chao Ho-hsan as ringleader, nursed a spirit of gaiety in all around them, telling stories, singing patriotic songs, tossing laughter between themselves like a shuttlecock. At night they stretched out wherever space permitted and told hair-raising ghost tales or engaged in endless discussions. Sometimes Thirty-nine wondered where their words came from as they argued about political and military leaders, social programs, the affairs of other nations, the comparative strength of Chinese and Japanese armed forces—all in the same breath.

Making him one of themselves, they would frequently call out, "Li, what do you think?" San-djiu would smile and say little, but he listened intently. If some of the talk seemed wild and foolish, much more was sound and informative. These fellows worked their minds as hard as laborers their bodies, he told himself, and from them much could be learned.

The students, in turn, were fascinated by Li's professional use of the medical supplies in emergencies. Even in the ordinary happenings of daily life, he was much more practical than any of them. "Li," they would call, "look a look at Ling's rickshaw!" or "Li, tell us the best way to repair Chang's load!"

Chinese country people learned in childhood to depend on their own wits and hands. San-djiu would study the trouble, scratch his head in the process of thinking, then say, *"Ko ee hsiang fa tz!* (Can think up a way!)" Since his companions were given to bestowing nicknames on each other, he soon became "Hsiang fa Li."

While the great surge in traffic was westward, occasional travelers arrived from that direction. Sometimes troops of soldiers appeared marching in formation toward the Eastern Front. Only then did the opposing jam of bodies scatter to clear the way. With an ingrained fear of military uniforms, the older generation was learning very slowly that National Government troops were different from any they had ever known. The students alone had no fears. Greeting the new-comers with patriotic slogans, they called out the eternal question, "What news?" Thus Li and his party learned sadly that the Yellow's dykes had been broken, and Hankow and Canton had passed into enemy hands.

The first information weighed heavily on Thirty-nine's mind. He was deeply concerned about Hsiao Pan. With Chi Farm flooded, where now would that one and his brother go? Li had the unhappy feeling that never again would he hear from this friend.

One evening in a small town midway to Chungking, the refugees met a group of wandering players. Many of the actors were boys and girls too young to serve the nation in other ways. Carefully chaperoned and coached, they jour-neyed all over China's vast countryside, devoting perform-ances to the business of waking up complacent citizens. War had not yet touched the western provinces, and populations felt far enough away from the Coast to have little interest in national unity. Speeches, printed matter, and even the radio broadcasting in Free China had done little to change hinterland viewpoints. No Chinese, however, could resist theatricals. These roving troupers, putting on old-fashioned as well as modern patriotic dramas, succeeded in stirring most audiences to active interest in national affairs.

Sometimes the highway neared the Yangtze, and the weary crowds paused to look far below the bronze and purple cliffs to a river that was as congested with craft as the road with pedestrians and vehicles. San-djiu wondered if the two physicians were aboard any of the steamers that struggled over the seething water and came slowly into view. His hope was that the others had long since reached Chungking, for he could not help but be anxious about arriving in that city. Weeks ago his party had crossed the border from Hupeh Province into Szechuen, and wherever the highway passed through villages or towns the refugees were made to feel the chill resentment of local inhabitants.

One morning in Wanhsien, having bought breakfast from a street vender, Li squatted to eat before the entrance to a large silk shop. Inside, employees were talking together. An accountant poised expertly reckoning fingers on the beaded wires of an abacus to remark impatiently, "Today there are even more strangers than yesterday."

"*Ai!*" came a response, "and before sunset how many? Like locusts these other-province people swarm into this city and in flight strip us bare as any grain field."

San-djiu wondered if the two physicians were aboard.

"You would have them stay down river to be killed by the short-legged ones?" reproached an older clerk. "True it is that Szechuen's winds are cruel to the naked and homeless!"

"No more than most men do I lack pity," the other muttered in defense, "but with rice almost twice its usual price and rents stretching to the sky—how can the head of a family know peace?"

Listening to this conversation, the proprietor felt his own mind divided by the same arguments—pity for the victims of war and concern over the threat they offered to Szechuen. By unceasing toil and effort through more than forty years had he founded and built his own business. Now, at sixty, he had no energy left with which to combat any threat, however slight, of social upheaval in this, his native province.

He turned to ask gravely, as an apprentice came in from the street, "Where does the Government send these—to Kweichow or Yunnan? Or do they stay here?"

"Honorable Merchant, I know absolutely nothing!" the boy replied. "For a time I stood on the curb to listen, but could understand little; many of these down-river people speak differently from us."

"All but those from around Shanghai use Guang Hwa (Mandarin, China's official language); yet even their Mandarin differs from Szechuenese," finished the owner.

"And the authorities expect them to live and work together like members of a family. 'Every hundred *li* the weather changes,'" the accountant quoted. "Are men less different?"

The kindly older clerk now advised, "Let us remember what the Generalissimo said on the Chungking radio. For the first time in history, East, South, North, and West work together against a common enemy. From every city on the Great Sea and on the Son of the Sea these people come to us in the west for refuge. Only by forgetting our differences can we continue as a nation!"

Digesting this with the food, San-djiu mused on the fact that the Government was already in Chungking. Something about that fact made him fear the strange city less. What these men in the silk shop had just said was true enough. Had many strangers come to the Point, Lao To and all the neighbors would have resented the newcomers bitterly. The Szechuenese were said to be powerful, wealthy, and proud. For years they had lived to themselves, giving no thought to the changing national capitals, so the students had told him. And now the Government and what must seem all the rest of China, as well, were forcing entrance through their doors. He must tell his companions what he had just heard, that they too might better understand.

On a cold and misty January morning, just eighteen months after being driven from his home on the Point, Li San-djiu-tz arrived in Chungking, Free China.

CHAPTER XIII

"Though They Drive Us Into Tibet, Still We Shall Return and Conquer!"—Generalissimo Chiang Kai-shek

IN CHUNGKING the bewildered horde of daily arrivals, having reached the first objective on the long journey, now asked wearily, *"Shang na li ch'ü? (Where do we go?)"*

The very air seemed alive with answers, for this ancient port had become a clearinghouse for a whole nation. "Go to Szechuen's Min River Valley! There the silkworms have two rearings a year. *China's silk will buy tanks and trucks from the rest of the world.*

"Go to Loshan for the culture of wax-bearing insects! *China's wax will purchase foreign airplanes.*

"Go to Kunming's forested mountains! *China needs wood for thousands of junks and vehicles.*

"Go to Sikang's rich farm lands! *Free China must now produce all her own food.*

"Go everywhere in these four western provinces—Szech-uen, Kweichow, Sikang, Yunnan! Make the tung trees yield oil! *China's tung oil will pay for American gasoline.* Dig into the earth for gold, silver, lead, tin, copper, nickel, coal, antimony and magnesium! *These will make China's munitions, fire her furnaces, finance this war.*"

Listening, the refugees found hope. In the eastern provinces food had never been sufficient; the overworked soil had cried for rest; the forests had long since disappeared. Men labored unceasingly for mere existence, battling the ever-recurring floods, droughts, and locust swarms. But beyond Chungking, it was said, fields waited to be tilled and forests to be cut, and no one spoke of rainless summers or of rivers in flood. Driven from their homes by the enemy, the fleeing-trouble-people had never really believed the Government promise of a new life in the West. Yet, there had been no place else to go, and after almost two thousand miles of journeying, they had arrived to find doubts swept away by facts.

Straightening tired shoulders, the newcomers trudged on to definite goals. There the starving were fed and the sick and aged given medical care. Children who had lost parents found haven in Madame Chiang Kai-shek's War Orphanages. And the able-bodied went to work! Financed by Government loans, new settlements sprang up like mushrooms after a long rainy season. In Co-operatives these began to produce almost at once, and the original debts were swiftly wiped out. This was Free China where the penniless had livelihood; the homeless, shelter; the unemployed, work.

Like everyone else entering Chungking from down river, San-djiu's companions, the students, asked, "Where do we go?"

They were directed at once to a town halfway to Chengtu, the provincial capital. Since Chu's leg was still in the splints, his comrades pooled resources and purchased him a ticket on a bus bound for the appointed place. At parting, the injured youth expressed his deep gratitude to Li. "But for you," he said with feeling, "I might still be eating my heart in Ichang! How can I ever repay this?"

"Too small an affair! Too small an affair!" Thirty-nine assured him. "Truly, your accident was my good fortune; otherwise I should have been one person alone in that crowd of refugees."

"Guest talk!" protested Chu; and Chao Ho-hsan, who never lacked words, added, "You are a good friend and we shall not forget your kindness." Then switching to nonsense, he pulled the spectacles down on the end of his nose and with mock seriousness promised, "When I become the General-issimo's first adviser, Li, you will be appointed to high official position!"

"You, Chiang Kai-shek's adviser—you appoint to official position!" hooted Chao's companions. "When the crow becomes a golden pheasant! When the fox grows into a tiger—ai-ya!"

Chao Ho-hsan looked from one schoolmate to another and shook his head pityingly. "Only the wise can recognize hidden merit. Some day, gentlemen, when you come to me begging favors, I will give you what our respected friends, the Americans, call 'the raspberry'!"

"Rassbelly is what?" San-djiu asked when the laughter subsided.

"A small fruit a little like *yang mei ko tz* (strawberry). Some grew in the garden at college and were very good to eat."

And what are *yang mei ko tz*? the fishing-youth, never having seen any, asked himself, then added aloud, "Giving fruit to others—why is that bad?"

"Li, even *I* do not know—it is just another queer foreign expression."

Later, watching Chao and the rest of the party pick up their burdens and disappear in highway traffic going toward Chengtu, Thirty-nine continued thinking about these recent companions. What he had said politely had been the truth —journeying with them for so long had been good in many ways and had helped him and a number of grief-stricken refugees on the road to laugh easily again. The result in his own case had been to make the experiences of the past eighteen months seem less grim.

At the Red Cross office Li found the expected note from Hu Ih-hseng. A clerk obligingly translated the contents, dated two months earlier, and in a short time the youth was on his way to the physician's address. This, in the second range of hills across the Yangtze from Chungking, had to be reached by ferry, then by a long climb through terraced fields.

Everywhere Thirty-nine looked, the countryside lay veiled in fog, for Chungking and its environs knew little sunshine

from November to March. He missed the bright blue skies
of the Yangtze and Yellow Valleys and the crisp, invigor-
ating cold of winter days. Here one shivered just as much,
but the cause was dampness and not low temperatures.

San-djiu found Hu Ih-hseng in a temporary office among
several partially constructed buildings, and for an hour or
more they talked of their respective trips. The old steamer
on which the physicians had been passengers had gone on a
rock in the Second Gorge. The accident had been close to
shore, so surprisingly few lives were lost. For a time the
two doctors had been kept busy taking care of minor injuries
among the rescued; and local people from a large village
halfway up the cliffs had supplied food and shelter for the
many unexpected guests.

Ten days later a junk anchoring near by for the night had
proved to be less crowded than most ships out of Ichang.
On it, at exorbitant rates, accommodations were found for
about fifty of the marooned travelers, including the physicians. The remainder of the trip on this vessel was slow
but very interesting, Hu Ih-hseng related. Trackers connected by long bamboo hawsers to the ship crawled along
narrow paths cut high in the side of the cliffs and pulled the
junk over the worst rapids and whirlpools. There had been
a few bad moments on the way, but Chungking had at last
been safely reached. The next day Meng Ih-hseng had left
for Kunming.

"The river people must fear strangers less than do the
Szechuenese on the highway," Li remarked when this account
ended.

"Naturally! In the Gorges rescuing the shipwrecked is a chief means of livelihood."

Thirty-nine repeated the conversation overheard in the silk shop at Wanhsien, and the listener nodded understandingly. "The refugees are no small problem for Szechuen. People here have always thought themselves better than other men, and now the National Government keeps reminding them that the citizens of all provinces are equally important." He chuckled suddenly and went on, "When I was a boy, Li, my old teacher told me an ancient tale of a Szechuenese scholar who when tested with other learned men at Peking, showed that his knowledge was much greater than theirs. Astonished, the examiners commented, 'Revered Sir, surely you must be the wisest man in your Province!'

" 'In Szechuen,' he contradicted, 'persons of my ability are as plentiful as grains in a load of millet.' "

Thirty-nine grinned and Hu concluded, "Nevertheless it is true that Szechuenese have many good reasons for their pride." Abruptly, the physician changed the subject, "Take off your jacket and let me look at that arm!" After a minute or two he stated, "As I feared, pulling a rickshaw was not too good. Did it pain much?"

"The first few days. Then Chu helped me make a tight bandage."

"A good plan! For a while use it little. Now listen: Several months will be needed to complete these buildings and still more time to get the equipment from America. Until everything is ready I cannot appoint you orderly and pay wages. There are many ways, however, for a strong youth to earn food money around Chungking, and you may sleep here on that cot."

"Honorable Doctor, already you have given me too much," San-djiu responded, thinking of the expensive boat fare from Hankow to Ichang.

The physician's eyes narrowed with humor, "I warn you: When you become orderly here, you will earn every cash twice."

Hu looked at his watch, a foreign object greatly admired by Thirty-nine. "Each afternoon," the owner said, "I go to the Work Together Camp (Co-operative) for Disabled Soldiers. Today suppose you accompany me."

The camp, composed of square dugouts cut beneath terraced fields of bean and cabbage, would have been difficult for a stranger to find. Each held about ten occupants—wounded soldiers whose injuries permitted no return to the Front. Unable to fight or earn normal livelihood, many of these men had grown desperate. Finally someone suggested that the Co-operatives working so successfully among refugees might do equally well for crippled veterans.

Put into effect, the plan was accomplishing excellent results. The soldiers, taught new skills suitable to their strength and handicaps, once more felt themselves useful citizens helping to supply the country's wartime needs.

Hu Ih-hseng's daily visit was to those with unhealed wounds and amputations, and it was apparent that they looked forward to his coming. On this occasion Thirty-nine was introduced as an orderly who had grown up with soldiers.

One of the men whose head was swathed in bandages stared at the visitor and asked in a peculiar tone, "Li Orderly, your native place is where?"

When this was answered, the questioner continued, "You are called San-djiu, yes, not yes?"

"Truly!, but how do you know?" Thirty-nine returned in surprise. The chatter in the hut abruptly ceased so that all might hear this conversation.

"When the Central Government at Nanking sent men to the Fort," the man with bandaged head went on, "I was among them and I saw you many times."

"To come so far and find someone from home is strange, indeed!" was all San-djiu could say.

"No, no!" several interrupted. "In Chungking men meet everyone they know—all China comes here."

After a moment Li asked, "The Lieutenant—what happened to him?"

"First, he is no longer a lieutenant. For special work at Taierchuang he was made a major in the Intelligence Service. Second," the speaker paused dramatically, "just five days ago the officer came to see some of us in this camp."

For the moment Thirty-nine was speechless, then he asked, "Is the Lieutenant—the Major still in Chungking?"

"Who knows?"

"And Ding—do you remember him?"

"Of a certainty! Old Ding died at Soochow."

Walking back to the doctor's office, the youth was so much interested in this linking of present to past that he kept murmuring, "Queer indeed! Too hard to believe!"

"Last week I felt the same," Hu Ih-hseng assured him, "when I met my cousin on White Elephant Street. His home is in Hongkong and for ten years I have not seen him."

In the following months San-djiu, working wherever he could find odd jobs to do about Chungking, never ceased to be astounded by the activity with which each street and alley hummed. Thoroughfares were crowded with load-bearers, rickshaws, pack animals, motor cars, sedan chairs, and the oversized handcarts pulled by four to six men.

Built on a rocky peninsula where the Lin and Yangtze rivers met, the city was like none the youth had so far seen. To reach it men crawled like flies up more than four hundred steps from the waterfront and found their journey just begun. For Chungking through thousands of years of wars, floods, and fires had climbed crazily up and down its hills on long and narrow flights of worn stone steps. Since everything had to be built on slopes, most structures hugged the rock and had one entrance only. Space had always been at a premium, and dwellings flimsy and ramshackle in design rose one on the other like the results of some builder's nightmare.

The Central Government had in recent times leveled many of these winding flights of stairs and laid wide paved roads in their place. Old houses and shops fronting on the new streets had been torn down and rebuilt with an eye to both appearance and utility. Chungking had always been the chief port for all this far-reaching Western world. Ancient flagstone roads and the Yangtze and the Lin, or *Little River* as it was called, had been her chief arteries of traffic. Now broad, modern highways twisted across hills and into valleys like silver threads in a pattern of brown and green embroidery, while overhead the new airlanes lay mysteriously hidden in the Szechuen sky. The waterways surged with craft of every description. All through the West, streams and river stretches formerly considered impassable had been cleared and widened by dynamiting. Countless improvised rafts and cargo boats now floated on these to greater channels.

With only hills and rivers to choose from, the Government had placed Chungking's airport on a sand spit in the middle of the Yangtze. From this unusual site planes shuttled constantly to and from points north, west, south, and southeast. For Free China, unlike the one of former days that had always acted slowly and deliberately, was breathless with haste. Time was a priceless treasure—time in which to move a nation; to mobilize industries, stabilize finances, unify the people; time to acquire the munitions for continued resistance against an enemy that had been preparing for this war through many years.

Modern highways were the answer to urgent need, whether by land or air. The ten-day journey to Chengtu could now be made in ten hours by car and in eighty minutes by plane. Newer, shorter roads was the Generalissimo's insatiable demand of engineers. "A ten thousand *li* way to Russia that munitions may be obtained!" At once a half million coolies began to dig across the cold and barren northwest plains.

"A modern link to Burma to keep open a trade route with America and Europe!" And from Szechuen to the Burmese border every hamlet and village became responsible for part of the work. With farm and household tools and little else, they cut through whole mountain ranges. Men chiseled and dug; women hauled earth away; grandparents and children crushed the rock to roadbed size. Each household contributed service free as a gift to the nation, and in return their names were written on the Burma Road for all posterity to read.

In time San-djiu was to become familiar with most of the highways linking Chungking to the rest of the world. As Hu Ih-hseng had foretold, there were many opportunities here for a strong youth, running errands for merchants, unloading ships, helping boatmen pole sampans. And the jobs paid well, for workers were now earning wages greater than any they had ever received.

The wet, gray winter wore on, and the period of Excited Insects (mid-spring) ushered in a succession of days in which the burning sun seemed only a few feet above men's heads. The change in the weather was startling. One bright April day as Li helped five others pull a handcart loaded with tins of gasoline to an army training camp outside Chungking, he remarked, "Truly, it is good to have clear weather!"

The men laughed, and the eldest quoted, "When the sun comes out in Szechuen, the dogs begin to bark!" Then the speaker asked, pointing to lush fields of green vegetables and gold mustard, "In East China do crops this early look like those?"

"No," Thirty-nine admitted honestly.

"So I thought! Thus Szechuen fogs help the soil."

That the present year's long cloudy season had saved many of their lives the people were soon to discover. From the

"Truly, it is good to have clear weather!"

third of May until early November, punishment such as no
city in the world had ever endured from the air fell on
Chungking's defenseless head.

Li no longer sought jobs. With Hu Ih-hseng he was on
duty endlessly in the ravaged capital, helping to remove
citizens from falling buildings, giving First Aid, carrying
the injured to safety as had been done after the bombing at
Y——. But in comparison with this the destruction at
Y—— seemed child's play. Within the first few days of
bombing more than five thousand people died. At the Generalissimo's orders half the population was temporarily evac-
uated to the countryside, and the city began feverishly to
rebuild.

Possessing almost no fighter planes or antiaircraft guns,
Chungking still held two natural advantages over the enemy.
Tunnels dug deeply in her rocky foundation would, when
finished, provide raid shelters for a half million inhabitants.
Also, the invaders' nearest air base was several hundred
miles away and the flight over the mountains of Free China
was slow, difficult, and closely watched by Chiang Kai-shek's
lookouts.

Every Japanese air base in China had Chinese coolies
working on the field. If one of these laborers happened to
be a man of parts with a radio transmitter carefully concealed
in his tattered blue cotton garments, the arrogant conquerors
did not know it. As enemy planes took off for Chungking
the word flashed through to the Capital, and the air-raid signals began to operate. When the Szechuen boundary was
crossed, the first signal, large red paper balls (changed to

lanterns at night), rose on every hill and high building about the city. In about thirty minutes, after information had come that Chungking was the objective, a second ball appeared and a siren wailed shortly. Sometime later the final alarm found voice in a chorus of sirens, whistles, and foghorns. The balls came down, and when the "All Clear" sounded, a long green tube replaced them.

As civilians learned to recognize the importance of obeying signals and filing into shelters, the casualties from raids decreased to few in number. During that summer thousands of citizens had perished, and the modern streets and buildings scarred and gutted by fires and explosions, had become a mass of rubble. Yet Chungking continued much the same in spirit as she had been through all the centuries past— proud, stubborn, and undaunted. Just as fast as ruins could be cleared away, homes were rebuilt. Engineers filled in bomb craters and relaid thoroughfares. Fire fighters and public utilities workers never relaxed, scorning protection even while the successive waves of planes rained death into their midst.

As the people now went coolly into the rapidly increasing shelters, they called to each other, "Will Japan or China win this War?"

With magnificent assurance, the answer would come back, "Who does not know that?"

When the "All Clear" sounded and they began the painful searching for what once had been their homes, grimly philosophic citizens remarked, "If our houses are gone, the bombs that destroyed them cost Nippon more than the property was worth!"

On skeleton walls still standing they wrote the characters, "Japan did this and we must not forget!"

This determined air of courage among the persecuted Chungkingese, San-djiu told himself, was very different from the spirit in occupied areas. There, crushed under the aggressor's heel, even the stoutest-hearted patriots lived chiefly for vengeance. If some of the enemy could be made to suffer as they themselves had suffered, life itself was a cheap price to pay. But in the West men still breathed the air of freedom and the Generalissimo stood as a bulwark close at hand. Later they were to live by his challenge, "Let the enemy come! Let them drive us all the way to Tibet. Still I will return and conquer them!"

In November, when the first mists closed in about the city, Szechuenese hearts swelling with gratitude now spoke of their sodden skies as "Heaven's Blanket," for the raids lessened in number. Hu Ih-hseng was now spending more time again in the Hills. The medical buildings were nearly completed, but only a fraction of the equipment had yet arrived from abroad. Setting this up, however, needed his expert supervision and could not be trusted to artisans. Also, he was having a real problem trying to find a future staff for the institution, for doctors and nurses were at a premium.

One morning when the "All Clear" sounded after a minor air raid in which very little damage was done, San-djiu having found no profitable job in the city proper made his way down the long steps to the shore. There, surprisingly enough, was a real casualty—a cargo-carrying houseboat set aflame by bomb sparks. The boatman and his family had been rescued, but two of the crew were still struggling in the turbulent Yangtze. One of the men seemed to be losing strength, and Li, removing jacket and shoes, plunged into the river.

Accustomed to the buoyant sea, he found swimming in this fresh water unexpectedly difficult. At first the swift current carried him past his objective, but he managed to pull back in time and shortly the two were safe ashore. While the rescuer lay flat for a moment easing his lungs, a throng of spectators collected and made him the center of attention.

"Certainly your courage is great!" they assured him. "Have you no fear of the River Dragon, that you snatch prey from his jaws?"

"As a child I played with the Sea Dragon," San-djiu retorted, rising to his feet and looking for the discarded jacket and shoes.

The saved man now found breath to express deep gratitude, and after a polite phrase or two in response, the youth with possessions safe in hand made his escape from this highly embarrassing moment. Hurrying over the mud flat, he ran into an army officer going toward a ferry. Glancing up in swift apology, Thirty-nine felt words dying on his lips.

There before him the Lieutenant who had become Major exclaimed, in a well-remembered voice, "Li, can I believe my own eyes? How did you come to Chungking?"

CHAPTER XIV

"If You Strike at a Snake and Miss, Beware!"

AT FIRST, standing there before the officer, San-djiu could express his delight in a word of greeting only.

The Major, concerned about catching the ferry, asked hastily, "Do you stay in the city or across the river?"

"In the Hills, Sir."

"If you have no further duty in Chungking, come with me on this boat!"

The passengers already aboard opened a way for the officer and watched with frank interest as the youth with soaked cotton trousers and dry, faded jacket followed the well-groomed military figure. At once the two former acquaintances began to talk, and gradually the curious turned attention to other things.

"Now tell me how you came here!" ordered the Major.

Briefly Li outlined the circumstances leading to this moment.

Listening intently, his companion murmured sympathy over the loss of Lao To, then continued, "And at present what work do you do?"

"Sir, when the new hospital is ready, I am to be an orderly. Until that time I earn money in many ways around Chungking."

"You like orderly· duty?"

"Most, Sir, when the patients are soldiers."

"For the reason that you have always known army men!" The officer eyed him speculatively. "To find medical friends who would teach you such work was your great fortune. Moreover, Hu Ih-hseng is an excellent physician."

"Truly!" Thirty-nine responded enthusiastically. "Do you know him, Honorable Major?"

"No, but since he is to be superintendent of a military hospital, I have heard of him."

There was a moment of silence. Then the youth said hesitantly, "Once the Honorable Major told me that China depended on the young. I am older than many in the Army— perhaps I should be with them, not here."

"Our country has more than enough fighters, Li; medical workers are few. Thousands of soldiers die of small wounds because there is no one to care for them. Your hospital is also to train orderlies and nurses for the Front. If you can help Hu Ih-hseng with those beginners, that is a good way to serve the nation." The speaker gazed thoughtfully at the shore they were approaching. "What you do around Chungking, though, is *not* important." As the ferry arrived at the landing, he concluded, "You will hear from me again, Li."

Lost in thought, San-djiu followed the crowd from the boat and climbed slowly toward the second range. Ever since the soldier in the Work Together Camp had told of the Major's being in Chungking, the youth had longed to see the other once more. Hope of having the desire granted had not been very strong, for members of the Intelligence Division, it was said, lived strange and uncertain lives. To-day, with the wish fulfilled, Thirty-nine felt peculiarly light-hearted. The deep sense of loss that had possessed him after his grandfather's death seemed to have been eased by the recent encounter. Perhaps homesickness had been mingled with grief, and meeting the Major, a part of the old familiar scene, had lessened this.

From the first hour of acquaintance on the sea cliffs, Li had admired the young officer's courage and patriotism. True, the fishing-youth had experienced mixed feelings on the day when the other had so coolly shot the two Japanese and disposed of the bodies. At present, though, remembering Chi Farm, Y——, and, particularly, the past summer in Chungking—he felt much older than that untried boy from the Point. Who killed the "dwarfs" or how it was done no longer bothered him at all, for China was fighting an enemy as strong, cruel, and treacherous as any hungry tiger of the southern jungles.

Grateful and deeply interested as San-djiu was in the opportunity to work with Hu Ih-hseng, a good many times during the bombings of Chungking he had longed to carry a gun at the Front. Helping to pull from ruins the tortured bodies of men, women, and children, the young orderly, deafened by their screams of agony and soaked by their blood, had known an overwhelming need to strike back savagely at the aggressor. Only personal obligation to the physician who had done so much for him had kept Li from mentioning the longing before, and today the Major's statement about medical work had settled the matter completely.

At the hospital site, the physician could not be found, and Thirty-nine wandered over to the Work Together Camp. With the others in his cave, the soldier from the Fort was cutting out garments to be padded for the troops in winter campaigns. For a time the visitor helped by handing the workers tools and materials. After a while he announced, "This morning I met the Honorable Major on the opposite shore."

"*Ai-ya!*" exclaimed the soldier most concerned. "Did I not say that one would probably come again? If only the officer could tell us of his errands!"

Li grinned. "We are as likely to have a fish jump out of the Yangtze and ask, 'How are you?' " he replied.

Some time afterward Hu Ih-hseng arrived on his daily visit. Later, walking home with San-djiu, the physician said, "Just before I left for the camp, a friend of yours sent me a note."

"Honorable Doctor, you have heard from Meng Ih-hseng, not so?"

"Would that I had! No, the writer was the Major, courteously telling me of your meeting."

Thirty-nine was completely puzzled. Why should the officer write Hu Ih-hseng? This was queer, indeed! Aloud he said, "I came at once to tell the Honorable Doctor, then . . ."

Hu interrupted, "An official living here in the Hills invited me to look at his son. The boy does not thrive on the Chungking climate. Who does? Returning from the call, I found the letter from the officer. He wished to know whether at present I have great need for your services. If not, then the Government can use you until the hospital is ready. Early tomorrow you will go where the Major is staying in the First Range, and there learn more."

Li looked mystified. "The Government? I do not understand this affair. Also, Honorable Doctor, what do you wish me to do?"

"By note I told the Major that the hospital would not need you as orderly for two moons at least." Hu paused to study the youth's face. "You wish to go—not so?"

"Of a certainty!"

"That is fortunate," the other added with his familiar dry smile, "for the Army does not worry about men's wishes."

The rest of the day Li spent laundering garments and scrubbing shoes. Next morning, rising earlier than the usual hour at dawn, he gave himself the daily thorough washing that seemed the only way to repay Hu Ih-hseng for the privilege of sleeping in the office. With inward amusement—the youth admitted that these daily baths had actually become a pleasure—and that was too hard to believe.

Starting out, he passed through a village, and stopping at a food shop bought two fried twists of dough, smoking with grease. These were followed by a bowl of hot water, and a persimmon. The last luxury, split from over-ripeness, was purchased cheaply after much bargaining with the proprietor. When San-djiu continued on his way, with both hunger and business sense satisfied, he thought himself equipped to meet any situation.

This was fortunate, for one was immediately presented. At the given address, a well-clad servant of his own age eyed the newcomer from crown to toe and said coldly, "Your daring is great! Do you think one so important as the Honorable Major has time to waste?"

Thirty-nine felt suddenly as shabby and countrified as if still living on the Point. Then realizing that the fellow was only another farm boy in good garments, he regained assurance. "The Honorable Major sent me word to come here. In Szechuen do servants question their masters' affairs?"

How the argument uninterrupted might have ended remained a mystery, for a young officer now appeared, glanced at Li, and told the houseboy, "Take him inside at once!"

Aware of the servant's discomfiture, Thirty-nine, remembering Lao To's saying, "Courtesy is cheap; rudeness, costly," smiled as he followed the other down the hall. The next moment the episode was completely forgotten in listening to the officer.

"Yesterday," the Major began, "while we talked I recalled that you can do many useful things. The private who acted as my personal servant on the last journey must not soon be seen with me again. This time I thought you might like to go in his place."

Li's face was alight. "Most unworthy, Sir, most unworthy!" he managed to respond.

The officer rang for an aide, and when the other appeared, ordered, "Make arrangements with the usual tailor about an outfit for this man! Tell the sew-seam-one to send an apprentice at once to take measurements. By noon tomorrow the garments must be finished. Next, go to the Department of Education and get one of the boxes fitted to hold insect specimens and bottles of preservative solutions. I wish some specimens in the box—beetles, I think—and a book or two about them with good illustrations. Two mosquito nets will be needed, but no bedding or food. Later I will tell you about my clothing. Everything must go in one pigskin trunk."

When the aide had departed, the Major turned with a twinkle in his eye to Thirty-nine. "Do you know anything of beetles, Li?"

"No, Sir!"

"Nor I! Years ago I studied a little about them in the Mission High School but I have forgotten most of that. However, the subject is a safe one. There are so many kinds of beetles, some will be found wherever we go; and before returning, Li, both of us should know a great deal about them." The officer's voice became suddenly serious. "Now I must attend to other matters, but first, listen carefully! Do not mention me or this affair to anyone, even to Hu Ih-hseng—he will understand your silence. Tomorrow, be here before noon. These things you must remember on the road: I am Wang Chiao-hsou, a scientist from Chungking University who is writing a book on the beetles of Yunnan Province. You will always call me, Chiao-hsou (Sir, Teacher), *never anything else*. Also, I know nothing of the military; if we meet soldiers, we shall act like other civilians. That is all."

Later, having been measured for garments, Li wandered back to the hospital buildings. His thoughts were whirling. So the Major was taking him to Yunnan Province to study beetles! Well, he was glad that the officer—no, "Wang Chiao-hsou"—had chosen beetles and not the centipedes or lizards that every man in his race disliked. But whether centipedes or lizards or even snakes, what did it matter, since he was making this journey with the other?

Amusement welled within him at the thought of "Wang Chiao-hsou" studying beetles. For the first time since the war had started, San-djiu felt the burden of worry and depression slip from his mind. Somewhere on the road between Chungking and Kunming adventure waited—tempting and mysterious. What the officer's business in Yunnan might be, Li had no idea, but that it was concerned with something much more exciting than hunting beetles he was very sure.

The next day, having said farewell to Hu Ih-hseng, the youth went promptly to the appointment. There the young aide supplied him with the garments which Thirty-nine had not supposed any tailor could make in so short a time. Changing the old attire for these, he tied in his belt the money-bag containing small savings and the treasured letters from Hsaio Pan and the Captain to whom he had given blood.

Certainly the Wheel of Life turned strangely! When Hu Ih-hseng had first translated the Captain's letter and mentioned the address, Kunming had seemed in another world. Yet, today, he, Li San-djiu-tz, was starting on a journey to that very city. Well, he was still not likely ever to use the letter, but possessing it seemed queer just the same. Much more important was the possibility of seeing Meng Ih-hseng again. Having met in Chungking the Major and a soldier from the Fort, he believed now that anything might happen.

Properly clothed for travel and made responsible for the small trunk, Thirty-nine next found himself being carried over the countryside in a private car with the Major and a chauffeur. After the first exchange of greetings with his latest attendant, the officer discussed routes with the driver, and San-djiu studied his superior's transformation.

It was clear that the other was not *playing* the part of "Wang Chiao-hsou"; instead, he *had become* the scientist in every detail. Garbed in the conservative civilian robe and jacket of a college professor and wearing shell-rimmed spectacles, the erstwhile army man had disappeared completely. As was commonly the case with scholars who spent their lives poring over books or using microscopes, the other's shoulders were slightly rounded, and even his speech, Li soon discovered, was slower and more carefully phrased. If Thirty-nine had previously thought of the trip as light adventure, in the first few minutes he realized that the affair was entirely serious and a part of the deadly game of war.

The machine, making use of all available short cuts, proceeded at high speed day and night. The travelers slept in the car and stopped at settlements for meals only. In an extraordinarily short time they had crossed from Szechuen into Kweichow and neared the Yunnan border.

En route there was very little talking. In the daytime "Wang Chiao-hsou" was engrossed in the beetle books. Occasionally he showed Li illustrations or specimens from the case he carried. His only reference to the journey was that it was a pity college professors were so poor—otherwise the trip from Chungking to Kunming might have been made in a few hours by airplane.

San-djiu had never seen country so wild or beautiful. The car swept on between mountains, crossed narrow bridges over roaring streams, and came out again in lush green valleys. Old towns and villages were few in number, for the far southwestern provinces had been sparsely peopled by aboriginal tribes and a sprinkling of Chinese officials and businessmen.

At present modern highways linked the formerly isolated sections together, and crude young settlements were everywhere in evidence. Many of these had been formed by the refugees, and from the road their Co-operatives could be seen. To avoid attacks from the air, the Work Together establishments were always carefully camouflaged to look like surrounding fields or forests.

One forenoon the car came to a halt in a lonely country lane. The two passengers alighted with the luggage, and the chauffeur turned the machine around and started back to Chungking. When they were alone, the Major resumed his natural manner. "Yunnan Province, Li," he began, "is only a few hours distant. From here we return to the highway, walk south to the first village, and buy tickets on the bus to Kunming. In that city I want you to find me a room in one of the more recently built clean inns where bedding is supplied. The task will not be easy. The place is overcrowded, rooms are scarce, prices high, and 'Wang Chiao-hsou' has little to spend. When comfortably settled, we can begin to search for beetles."

Noticing a sudden flicker of amusement in Thirty-nine's eyes, the officer added, "Li, this beetle business is not humorous. Several East China colleges have moved to Kunming, and I would rather meet a battalion of the 'dwarfs' than one science professor." He caught up the small black case of equipment and said, "Now let us go on to that village."

On the highway a company of soldiers swung past them. These, young and fresh from a training camp, bore none of the marks of veterans. Clad in cheap cotton uniforms of blouses and shorts and poorly equipped, they marched gallantly along singing bits from the popular martial airs, "Our Nation Cannot Die" and "The Song of the Lone Battalion."

While the troops went by, "Wang Chiao-hsou" and his servant stepped to the side of the road. Watching them out of sight, the older man's eyes held an expression that had nothing to do with studious affairs. "Singing, they go to the Front," he said bitterly, "and to what purpose? To meet enemy airplanes, tanks, and artillery with hand grenades and rifles, and some of the rifles thirty years old! Then when their grenades and homemade cartridges give out, they will use rifle butts and stones, as some of our men have done on every battlefield in this war."

Only once or twice on the cliffs had Li heard the officer speak with such feeling. "But, Sir, I do not understand," he ventured. "The factories . . ."

"The factories," interrupted his companion, "cannot work magic. They are few in number and lack machinery for making big guns. Such things must be bought from America and Britain, and those nations are too busy selling munitions to Japan to squeeze heart over China's needs."

San-djiu was bewildered. Many times he had heard the two foreign countries, particularly America, referred to as China's friends. Hu Ih-hseng who had studied there, the students whose college had been supported by Americans— all had spoken in such terms. Furthermore, the three Americans he had known in the hospital at Y—— had been extremely anxious for the Generalissimo to win the conflict. The Government had even issued stamps with the flags of the two nations on them. Hu Ih-hseng had shown him one of these mailed from Kunming to Chungking. Yet, if America armed the "dwarfs," how could China consider it her friend? The question was too complicated for him to answer, and since the Major had already lapsed into somber silence, nothing more was said.

Arriving at the village, Li found a table in the teahouse for "Wang Chiao-hsou," saw that the other was satisfactorily served, then moved through the crowd of patrons toward the entrance. Perched on the low wooden grill work that ornamented the front, he gave his own order and listened to the conversations flowing about him. Close by were three men from a truck parked just outside. This, loaded with insect wax, was bound for Lashio on the Burma Road.

Interested in what they were saying about the journey, Thirty-nine remarked, "To drive that large a machine through these mountains must be difficult."

"*These* mountains!" exclaimed the driver. "Beyond, the country here seems like a plain; but tales of the road through Yunnan to Burma are too hard to believe for men who have never been there. One day, freeze on the peaks; the next, perish of heat and mosquitoes in the Salween Valley! And when rain falls, machines frequently slip over the precipices or are buried by landslides."

"Certainly great courage is needed to travel thus," the youth said admiringly.

"It is true the job is not for one with a chicken-liver," conceded the driver, "but the pay is very good, so *muh iu fa tz*!"

"Even in the rains the work is better than carrying wax insects as I formerly did," one of his helpers said.

Curious, Li asked, "Where did you take them?"

"From Sikang to Lohsan in Szechuen."

"For what reason?"

The three stared at him, then the driver inquired, "From what place do you come that you know nothing of these insects which make the finest wax in the world? I thought your speech was not of the West, though at present our ears are filled with so much strange language, sometimes we do not recognize our own."

San-djiu explained.

"From the Coast!" they chorused. "Truly you have journeyed a long way. And your business here?"

"Personal servant for Wang Chiao-hsou, a professor from Chungking University who hunts beetles," was the reply.

"Beetles!" The men looked questioningly from one to the other. "Why would anyone spend heart searching for bugs save those that trouble the body?" asked the helper who had hitherto been silent.

The former carrier of wax insects gestured expressively. "How can ignorant men like us hope to understand scholars?"

A small serving boy now brought Li's food, and the new acquaintances made room for the youth at their table. While he ate, San-djiu begged, "Please tell me more of the wax insects."

Hastily the story was pieced together. In Sikang and on the Yunnan-Szechuen border where the wax bearers grew and deposited scales full of eggs, they did not make wax. Why, no one knew; perhaps a scarcity of the necessary evergreen and ash trees was the cause, for several hundred miles away in Szechuen the insects never failed to cover such trees with the valuable deposit.

"And that is very good for the Szechuenese who miss no ways to earn silver," said the driver, adding in explanation, "I myself am a Kweichow man."

The least talkative among them smiled and repeated an old saying, " 'When other excitement is lacking, watch Kweichow and Szechuen pull skin (quarrel).' "

"In this affair," the third man remarked to Thirty-nine, "Szechuen's fortune is only seven-tenths good, for the winters there are too cold and the eggs perish. Early in spring Szechuenese merchants journey south to buy the eggs, and send them to Lohsan for resale to farmers. When the creatures hatch, they are placed on trees, where they make every twig and branch as white as snow in three months. The wax scraped off, boiled, and molded, is what fills that truck," he finished, and reached for his bowl of tea.

"I am very stupid," San-djiu persisted, "but why was carrying the insects so hard?"

"Because the journey needed almost twenty days, no matter how fast a man went," explained the one who knew from experience. "Even a few hours' delay would ruin the whole load. If the eggs began to hatch, the tiny insects covered the carriers, crawling into eyes, nose, ears, and mouth. No man could endure such torment, and the baskets had to be emptied by the roadside. Now most merchants send the scales swiftly by truck." He paused. "*Ai*, when I remember those pests, this work is a pleasure!"

Bus patrons were filing out to the highway and Li, politely bidding the truckmen farewell, made his way to the side of "Wang Chiao-hsou."

Two days later professor and servant reached Kunming, the ancient capital of Yunnan Province. Previously known as Yunnanfu, the city was beautifully located on a high plateau, surrounded by lakes that reflected the colorful and ever-changing sky. At present, though, the population found little leisure to admire the scenery, for Kunming was crowded beyond description. In contrast to Chungking, where motor vehicles were comparatively few, this great terminal for the

Burma Road was jammed with trucks. Those going southwest carried China's products to Lashio, and there picked up for the return trip foreign munitions forwarded from Rangoon.

Truck drivers and helpers moving about stalled machines jostled each other in Kunming's business section. Roughly they demanded gasoline, engine service, tire repairs, or an open road toward their destinations. Already striving desperately to care for the thousands of East China students and factory workers who were rebuilding their establishments here, the old city was completely overwhelmed by the Burma Road traffic.

As the officer had foretold, finding a decent room was not easy, and only after hours of search was a place located in a small inn just outside the city. Thirty-nine himself was glad to stretch out at night with several others on some bare planks placed on trestles in the inn kitchen. Good food was not to be had anywhere, but if the Major found inconveniences great, he did not mention the matter. And Li, used to discomforts all his life, was too much interested by the exciting activity about him to waste thought on anything else.

Against this clamorous background "Wang Chiao-hsou" and his servant now began the quiet, leisurely pursuit of collecting beetles. For perhaps ten days the excursions were always west on the Burma Road. There courteously asking permission, the beetle professor moved about farmyards or in fields close to the highway. He seemed particularly interested in disabled trucks; and wherever a gathering crowd indicated one of these, "Wang Chiao-hsou," hugging his specimen case, soon appeared. Bending over in a grassy ditch, he would come up with a trophy, open his box, and proceed at once to put the beetle in a solution. This unfamiliar process never failed to draw the interest of the Yunnanese country people from the all too common affair on the road.

Thirty-nine sometimes squirmed inwardly over such concentrated attention, but "Wang Chiao-hsou" remained unaffected. In a slow, scholarly way, he imparted information about his subject. Sticking the blade of a small knife into the door frame of a building, he would expose channels eaten by narrow black beetles or by white ants (termites). Often specimens obligingly emerged as illustrations, causing the fascinated listeners to exclaim, "Truly, here is a learned man who is still young—a rare thing indeed!"

"Wang Chiao-hsou" seemed especially interested whenever a bad tire caused trouble on a truck. Few machines possessed extra parts of any sort, and the disgruntled driver and helpers would carefully unload the vehicle in order to jack up the rear. Resting on some large case they had set beside the road, the scientist would rearrange specimens, write items in a little notebook, and engage in conversation with the men. During such talks both truckmen and professor learned many things.

After a time the beetle hunters remained in and around Kunming. "Wang Chiao-hsou" was now concerned in finding specimens that foraged at night, and he and his attendant did not set out on present expeditions until sunset. The routes chosen were, like the previous ones, close to the highway. Some of the same trucks met by the professor on the

This unfamiliar process never failed to draw interest.

road below Kunming had reached the city only to be held up by further difficulties. Recognizing scholar and servant, the truckmen would call out greetings and inquire about the search. "Wang Chiao-hsou" took pains to answer all questions and to wish workers better luck on the rest of the journey.

On night forays, the professor resorted to a flash light for aid in capturing field specimens. Every once in a while as he talked with the crews, he flicked on and off the mechanism of the little light in an absent-minded way. Vehicles and men were spotlighted eerily, and an occasional surly truckman complained of the light and muttered in the professor's hearing uncomplimentary remarks about lunatics. Li, aware that his superior did nothing without a purpose, wondered what was at the bottom of the whole performance.

On a side road about a *li* north of Kunming was a hamlet with a small and dingy inn. For each of five consecutive nights the beetle hunters found a deserted truck parked opposite this hostelry. Vehicles carrying valuable and dangerous cargoes were rarely left alone, and to have five different machines so neglected seemed peculiar. The fifth evening as Li, on hands and knees, chased a clicking beetle through the grass, a short man emerged from the inn opposite, glanced carefully about, then climbed quietly into the body of the truck. As he did so, the beams of the flash light flickered over him.

"What affair is this?" demanded the new arrival sharply.

"A thousand pardons, Sir," replied the professor. "My servant and I hunt night beetles with the light, and you startled me."

"Better it is you do not get in the way of workers," the other suggested brusquely. Murmuring further apology, "Wang Chiao-hsou" with his attendant retreated down the road toward Kunming. A safe distance away the two sank behind a protecting screen of greenery and the older man said, "In a few minutes, Li, we must creep back to watch."

"Sir," Thirty-nine interrupted, in a voice harsh with excitement, "the man in that truck is a Japanese."

"What?"

Hurriedly the youth sketched the tale of the Buddhist priest and finished, "As your light fell on his face, I recognized him, but I was not ten-tenths sure. Always before, he had worn a priest's robes; those working garments and longer hair made a difference. But as soon as he spoke, I knew."

For a moment the silence between them was pregnant with thought. Then the Major asked, "Li, you did not see him clearly—how can you be sure?"

"Sir, I know it is the same man," the youth maintained stoutly. "Had he seen my face, his eyes would have told the truth."

From the distance the two could hear a faint but distinct sound of ripping wood. Apparently the Japanese was busy at work opening cases. "This affair," the Major explained after a moment of listening, "is too important to permit mistakes. As you have guessed, I am not hunting beetles; instead, I am trying to discover who tampers with munitions in Yunnan and sends them on defective to Chungking. Among the hundreds of trucks we have met, ten or eleven bore a small strange code sign on the tailpiece, but there was no

damage to the cases in their cargoes before they reached
Kunming. That I found out whenever such vehicles had to
unload. Also, the drivers of those machines were always
rude when we approached; the others were not. Each of the
five trucks in this village has had the suspicious symbol; since
they were deserted as well, I became more certain the damage was being done here. The manner of this man tonight
seems only another proof."

He ceased speaking for a second or two, then went on.
"Catching the bribed truckmen will be simple—I have descriptions of the marked machines, and Chungking will
soon discover who are the traitors' assistants. What is still
to be learned, though, is the name of the Number One Man
in the case. Wang Ching-wei has a few paid agents in every
province, including Yunnan. Should that fellow be Japanese,
he himself may be the leader in Kunming. You and I could
capture him without too much difficulty, but if others come
to his assistance, he might escape or be killed. Neither must
happen—what the spy can tell us is too valuable."

Li was listening intently, and the Major continued as if
thinking aloud, "Equally important, I dare not let Yunnan
officials know who I am. One or two have not yet assured
the National Government of personal loyalty. Because of
these men, the ones who are loyal are very sensitive. To
have the Generalissimo send me here secretly on this errand
would make them lose face—and that would mean more
trouble for Chungking."

"There is one official in Kunming who might help," San-
djiu offered slowly; "his son is a captain in the Army."

"Li, what nonsense is this?" the Major exclaimed impatiently. "First you know a Japanese spy—then an official with an officer son—who else?"

"Nobody, Sir. In the hospital at Y——, I did a small favor for that Captain. Here is a letter to his family."

Cautiously shielding the flash light against the ground, the officer read, and exclaimed, "Tonight the gods are certainly with us! This man Yen is one of the Governor's chief advisers. You know, of course, where the official residence is?"

"Yes, Sir. My first day in Kunming, I looked for the place. In a few minutes I can run there."

"Then go at once! Tell the gateman you have a letter for that official and refuse to see anyone else. When you have told your story, ask for help in taking the spy prisoner. That is the first thing to be done. Remember, *you alone* are interested in his capture; 'Wang Chiao-hsou' is not. Now hurry, for the truck may not remain there long."

CHAPTER XV

"China Ten Thousand Times Ten Thousand Years!"

WHEN San-djiu knocked at the entrance to the official residence, the gateman at first refused to open. Only the repeated statement about an official matter of great importance finally made him change his mind. When the man caught sight of Li, he exclaimed, "You do not wear the livery of Government servants—what is your business at this hour?"

"I have a letter for Yen Official. I myself wish to give it to him."

The gateman dismissed the last sentence with a grunt. "Give me the letter! We observe the proprieties in this establishment. Do you think the Honored Ones inside these gates permit nobodies from the street to bother them?"

Li took the letter from his belt, pulled out the folded sheet, and thrust the empty envelope in the other's hand. "Please show that to Yen Official at once. Tell him I hold a letter from his son, the Captain."

"Yen Captain—what do you know of him?" asked the gateman, lifting his lantern and looking again into Li's upturned face.

"Enough—please hurry! The matter is supremely important!"

Within a few minutes, San-djiu was led into a reception hall and left with a dignified, elderly man who now said, "This envelope belongs to a youth in the distant city of Y——. Where did you get it?"

Li was so concerned about the passage of time that his natural timidity in dealing with an important personage disappeared. "Respected Yen Official, the Honorable Captain gave me this letter," he said, handing it over. "I am the orderly he mentions in Y—— hospital."

The official read, then eyed the youth steadily. "Describe Yen Captain's appearance; also, why was he a patient in that Healing Hall?"

When the proper answers had been made, the questioner continued, "The names of his doctors?"

"Meng Ih-hseng and Hu Ih-hseng, Honorable Sir," was the reply.

Evidently satisfied about Li's identity, Yen Official inquired, "How did you come to Kunming?"

"Last January, Honorable Sir, I reached Chungking and half a moon ago arrived here with 'Wang Chiao-hsou,' a professor from Chungking University who writes a book on the beetles in Yunnan. Tonight something important happened."

"What?"

San-djiu explained about the Japanese spy.

"You are young and sometimes the young make mistakes. Are you certain this is the same man?"

"Ten-tenths, Respected Official. Since he did great harm at Y——, I thought the government here should know."

The official seemed to be pondering the matter, then he said, "To arrest him is a small matter; if innocent, he can be freed again. What does that truck carry?"

"Gun cases, Sir!"

"So! We must learn the name of his superior, for he cannot do such work alone. The situation is unusual, but it shall be attended to at once. I wish you to remain here until the prisoner appears."

Since Wang Chiao-hsou expected his attendant to return with help, this plan of the official's presented a problem. However, the Major was undoubtedly used to surprises, and, Li supposed, would be quite equal to this one.

After Yen Official had sent off his men with detailed instructions, the youth was ushered into another room and there served tea and sweetmeats. Time seemed endless in passing, though it was really only a half hour before the servant reappeared and led him back to the reception hall. Four guards stood with the prisoner before the official. As San-djiu entered through a door facing the captive, the Japanese started, muttered an imprecation, then lapsed into stony silence.

This revelation was all Yen Official needed. He murmured some orders to the chief guard, and when the bound man had been taken away, said to Li, "You may go now and come back in the morning. By that time our spy will doubtless have told all we wish to know."

Dismissed, San-djiu hurried first to where he had left "Wang Chiao-hsou," but the professor had already returned to his room. There a little later the two, recounting individual experiences, put the whole story together. "Wang Chiao-hsou," hidden in the grass, had not been too surprised by his servant's failure to return. The guards had done the job very neatly. There had been some noise, of course, and the professor had expected truckmen to rush from the dingy inn and help the "dwarf." But these were probably engrossed in a game of *mah pai*, for nothing had happened.

"Sir," Li said at the end, "one question I would ask: You spoke of a small code sign on the trucks—who put it there?"

"Someone between Kunming and Lashio, thereby making it easy for the traitors here to recognize co-operating machines. If Yen learns that the Japanese does not work alone in this city, the rest will be easy. A man who betrays his country, Li, will readily betray other men. Now go sleep before the cooks chase you from the kitchen."

On his return to the official residence the following morning, Li was told that the spy had eventually named a merchant in Kunming as his chief. He shivered at the thought of how this confession must have been accomplished. The merchant, warned by a guilty truck driver of the "dwarf's" strange disappearance, had prepared at once to leave Kunming by airplane. Arrested on the airfield the traitor, under pressure, had been glad to divide the blame with a man in Wanting.

Having courteously informed the eager youth of these developments, Yen Official added that the Yunnan Government was taking care of the matter and neither the Japanese nor his accomplices would ever trouble China again.

Li tried with difficulty to express his gratitude.

"All of our name owe you much," Yen Captain's father had replied. "When you first came here I thought that we were being given a chance to repay the debt. Instead, we are now more obligated than before. Any opportunity to destroy China's enemies is worth a great deal." The Official smiled. "In youth, one has many wishes. What is yours?"

San-djiu bowed. "To catch that spy was my only desire, Respected Sir. Soon I return to work in the new military hospital at Chungking. Since I am the only one left of our family, my needs are few. Truly, Honorable Yen Official, I am most unworthy of your kindness."

Several days later "Wang Chiao-hsou" and his servant traveled homeward from Kunming to Chungking by bus. As far as the Major was concerned, the assignment was already in the past, and he was anxious to reach the Capital to report. Others in Government service would apprehend and punish the guilty truckmen. It would be interesting to know what had prompted the men involved to become traitors. Some probably had relatives in Occupied Territory, and in such cases Japan had undoubtedly threatened persecution of hostages to force co-operation. Also, running a truck on the

Burma Road was a grueling occupation, and every one of those drivers and helpers knew that each trip might cost his life. For relaxation from strain, these men spent the nights in terminals and stopovers gambling away earnings. For the losers in such games, bribes of money presented tremendous temptation. Well, whatever their reasons for betraying China, they would all pay for the act with their lives. In war only weak and foolish governments excused treachery.

For Li, who looked forward to less exciting occupation than work in the Intelligence Division, the events in Kunming furnished great mental satisfaction. His stay in the ancient city had lacked only one thing, meeting Meng Ih-hseng again. At the Medical Commission Headquarters, he had been told that some of the physicians were remaining in the Salween Valley where the malignant malaria was worst, and Doctor Morland was among these.

Arriving in Chungking, the two travelers went first to the Major's private quarters. There the professor promptly dropped disguise, and said with customary humor, "Li, that 'Wang Chiao-hsou' has had so successful a trip is due largely to his unusual attendant. After you recognized the spy and showed me the letter to Yen, I should not have been surprised to see you try the mango trick.

"Since Hu Ih-hseng," the officer continued, "was also interested in the spy, you may tell him about that affair and the letter. Do not mention the business of 'Wang Chiao-hsou' who is now going to die a scholarly death. His rare collection of beetles will be bequeathed to the Education Department." In a graver voice the Major concluded, "Li, a man in the Army would be honored by higher rank for the work you did at Kunming. As it is, I can merely thank you deeply in the name of the National Government. In the future I shall expect to see you often. Now go to your doctor friend at the hospital and as you help him train new orderlies, remember *Chung Kuo wan wan sui!* (China ten thousand times ten thousand years!)"

Shortly afterwards, making his way home to the medical buildings, Li felt happier than ever before in life. He had worried about not being with the troops, yet today the Major had thanked him in the name of the National Government for assistance in Kunming. That the Japanese had been in Yunnan at the time, Thirty-nine realized, was his own good fortune and little else. Well, the affair had turned out very well, and the letter to Yen Official, which he had never expected to use, had proved very valuable. What warmed his heart more than anything else was the Major's parting remark. He, Li San-djiu-tz, had been ordered back to duty in the hospital with the cry of Chinese troops going into battle, *"Chung Kuo wan wan sui!"* Should he ever again long for service more exciting than that in the Healing Hall, the memory of this challenge would soon overcome discontent.

Li found the hospital buildings completed and Hu Ih-hseng busily unpacking the last of the long-awaited equipment, which had arrived only the preceding day. At once the youth began to help, and as they worked together, he related the story of the spy.

"Good news, indeed!" Hu exclaimed. "Many times I have wondered what evil the fellow might be doing elsewhere in this land."

Within a month the new military hospital was functioning, and San-djiu found his duties increasing daily. One morning the physician called him into the office. "Li," he said, "each day I want you to study one hour with a teacher, for the few characters I have taught you are not enough. There is no need to become a scholar, but you can learn the simplified language without difficulty. When you know that much, these other orderlies who come from schools will respect you more. This is important, since I wish to give you greater responsibility."

The first lesson occurred on the following afternoon. As the book knowledge was gradually acquired, Thirty-nine felt self-respect increase. For a fisherman, learning had seemed unnecessary to life; now time and circumstances had completely changed this former viewpoint.

Old moons died and crescents rose. An unceasing stream of wounded passed in and out the *Ih-yuen,* and every few months a new class of orderlies went to the Front. Periodically the Major reappeared at his quarters in the Hills and sent for Li for a brief visit. At the close of the first hospital year, much to Hu Ih-hseng's delight, Doctor Morland arrived with the Commission to report to the Government. The party returned to Yunnan by airplane the following day, but the two physicians sat all night and talked. To San-djiu the American found time to say, "You have grown five inches, Li, since I left you in Ichang. And Hu Ih-hseng tells me that you

caught your spy and went all the way to Kunming to do it!"
This was followed by a warm exchange of questions about
each other's welfare, and a brief discussion of the war.

While these personal contacts were adding special interest
to Thirty-nine's life as orderly in the new institution, Chungking itself went on with the increasing program of activity
from one year into another. Regularly with the return of
good weather the city received its familiar punishment from
the air, but conditions in this third season of bombing were
very different from those in that summer following Li's arrival. Due to the destruction of her ancient streets and buildings, Chungking was being made over into a more modern
capital with wide streets and broad fire lanes in which incendiary bombs could be swiftly quenched. Citizens pointed
to civic improvements and commented sardonically, "The
Japanese did this for us and at great expense to themselves!"

Now when raid signals came, people put their daily affairs
in order and in calm, leisurely fashion entered the shelters.
As a result, few lives were lost, and while some property was
still destroyed, new buildings promptly took the place of
the old. Refugees and war orphans were being cared for in
ever larger groups; and students educated, not only for front
line service as in other countries, but to take up the problems
of civilian life at the War's end. China's women led by
Madame Chiang Kai-shek, were breaking traditional bonds
thousands of years old, and helping in every line of civilian
work. Many had already gone straight to the Front as nurses
and helpers with the forces.

In industry, the factories, seriously handicapped by lack of machine parts, were functioning with only the greatest difficulty. Attempting to make up for this loss, thousands of Co-operatives worked day and night to produce everything from guns and ammunition to soap and blankets. Yet in spite of this desperate striving to supply her own needs China was slowly but surely losing ground to the aggressors.

The reiterated pleas to the outside world to hurry munition purchases seemed to fall on deaf ears. Great Britain was fighting a war in Europe; for the same reason Russia would soon be compelled to curtail the supplies reaching Chungking over the barren northern road. Airplanes from America were what the Generalissimo needed most, and in anticipation airfields dotted unoccupied areas everywhere. In ghostly quietude, the bare, level runways lay through blazing summers and freezing winters—waiting, waiting for the machines that did not arrive. Yet Chiang Kai-shek never lost faith in the outcome of the War. With unfaltering belief in the righteousness of his people's cause, he led the nation hopefully toward the day of victory.

One, two, three, and then four years of the conflict had passed, and China, unprepared and ill-equipped from the beginning, still held her powerful enemy at bay. Civilians as well as soldiers had died by the millions, but those who were left fought on with redoubled efforts. Winning only a few major battles, regular troops and guerrillas had managed somehow to account for a million and a half of Japan's best fighting men. And still the War went on.

When the fifth year of fighting was five moons old, word came that America and Britain, with other smaller nations, had been provoked into war against Japan. Now at last China who had been fighting alone so long had allies, the people told themselves. Now at last the bitterly needed airplanes and big guns would certainly come!

Their joy was short-lived, for elsewhere Japanese successes were swiftly achieved. The Philippines, Singapore, The Netherlands East Indies, Burma—all fell like rich jewels into the aggressors' greedy, blood-encrusted hands. And with each victory Japan found the thought of undefeated China increasingly bitter. With the closing of the Burma Road, Chungking was cut off from the outside world by land and sea. Yet, in spite of isolation, the Generalissimo was already building another highway through the ranges of India; and his troops had won a decisive battle at Changsha.

In the sixth summer of the invasion, the enemy opened new fronts in China, and the bombings of Chungking were again intensified. On one of these occasions the military hospital in the second range of hills was hit. Fortunately no patients were inside, for all had been carried into shelters before the final warning siren wailed. When the "All Clear" sounded, though, the wing containing Hu Ih-hseng's special pride, the surgery, was a mass of wreckage. For the rest of the day and through the following night, the physician, helped by Li and other workers who could be spared from routine duties, strove to clear away the mass of rubble. At dawn the physician ordered a halt in the work and went to his office. There a little later San-djiu followed, hoping for words with which

to express sympathy about the loss of the valuable foreign equipment. Hesitatingly he knocked on the door,
then entering found the doctor bent over drawings on his
desk.

The youth murmured what was in his heart, and the other
glanced up with a tired smile. "They are gone, Li, and we
dare not hope for replacements from abroad. Some time ago,
fearing this very thing, I planned some substitutes. There is
a clever ironworker over in the city, and he will help me
make duplicates of a few articles. They will be rough and
crude and harder to use, but they will serve, I believe, and
that is most important." He paused, then changed the subject, "You had better bathe and get three hours sleep before
returning to duty."

Thirty-nine walked out into the cool morning air. In the
east the sun was rising, and the light touched the tops of the
purple ranges stretching away to Yunnan and Burma. Doubtless he would always long for the sea, but the mountains and
valleys of this far western world had now become home and
these courageous Szechuenese his neighbors. No longer was
he one person alone, facing the future without relatives or
friends. Five years had passed since the bombing of the
Point, and in that time the slender boy had become a stalwart
man. Free China was now his family, and men like the
Major and the Doctor were enriching life with friendships
such as the fishing youth had never even imagined.

As he stood there in the brightening light, the thought came
to him that Hu Ih-hseng's way was China's way. Lacking almost everything that was needed to preserve the nation in

this conflict, still his countrymen had found means of going on with the task.

"Rough and crude and harder to use," the physician had said of the equipment he planned to make. Well, Chinese were used to difficulty and to suffering also. The Major had told Li of troops who had been without food for two days winning in an encounter with well-fed Japanese. Everywhere his people starved and fought and died for one purpose—to be free. And if no help came from outside and the nation went down to defeat, they would still die as free men, and not as slaves.

The sun was climbing swiftly above the horizon, which meant more bombings today. Surely sometime the night of war would pass and dawn once more bring peace to this tormented land. Weary and begrimed, Li San-djiu-tz stood for a moment longer in the radiant light. *"Chung Kuo wan wan sui!"* he whispered, then again more firmly and hopefully, *"Chung Kuo wan wan sui!"* With head up and shoulders lifted, he turned and moved toward his quarters in the hospital.

PRONUNCIATIONS AND NOTES

PAGE

131	Ih Yung Chun	ē yŭng chŭn
137	Ya-men	yä-mŭn
140	Me-me	mā-mā
140	Je-je	jā-jā
142	ho-chae	hō-chā
148	Hsien Chang	shĕn jäng
154	Ch'a puh do	ch'ä bŭh dō
177	Sun Yat-sen	sŭn yät-sen
177	Hu Shih	hōō shĕ
186	Taierchuang	tīêrchwäng
194	T'ao Yuan-ming	t'ou yūän-mĭng
201	Szechuen	sĕchuän
205	Hwang Ho	hwäng hō
206	Yunnan	yōōĭnnăn
208	Hanyang	hănyäng
208	Wuchang	wōōchäng
211	Chao Ho-hsan	chou hō-săn
211	ting hao tih ren	ding hou di ren
215	ko ee hsiang fa tz	kō ē hsăng fä dz
215	Hsiang-fa Li	hsăng-fä lē
216	Hupeh	hōōbŭh
216	Wanhsien	wänshĕn
218	Kweichow	gwäjō
218	Guang Hwa	gwäng hwä
220	shang na li ch'u	shäng nä lē ch'u
221	Sikang	sĭkäng
222	Chengtu	chĕngdōō
223	yang mei ko tz	yäng mā gō dz
243	Wang Chiao-hsou	wäng jou-shōō
248	Lashio	läshēō
248	Lohsan	lōsàn
250	Yunnanfu	yōōinnănfōō
256	Wang Ching-wei	wäng jĭng-wā
264	Chung Kuo wan wan sui	jŭng gwŭ wän wän swā
268	Changsha	chängsha